The
WENTWORTHS

ALSO BY KATIE ARNOLDI

Chemical Pink

The WENTWORTHS

a novel

Katie Arnoldi

THE OVERLOOK PRESS
New York

This paperback edition first published in the United States in 2009 by

The Overlook Press, Peter Mayer Publishers, Inc.
141 Wooster Street
New York, NY 10012
www.overlookpress.com

Cataloging-in-Publication Data is available from the Library of Congress

Book design and type formatting by Bernard Schleifer
Manufactured in the United States of America
ISBN 978-1-59020-152-7
10 9 8 7 6 5 4 3 2 1

To my wonderful family

(who are nothing like the Wentworths)

and especially to

Chuck, Ryland, and Natalie

Meet the Wentworths

———

They're standing in a police station somewhere in Los Feliz. It's three in the morning, cold and hostile. The fluorescent lights buzz. The guard on duty scribbles in a logbook and drinks his coffee. No one speaks. The mother clutches the father's arm; the oldest son stands off to the right with his arms folded across his chest. The daughter leans in close to her mother while the son-in-law stands behind, patting his wife's shoulder, wishing she would lean on him for support once in awhile. Judith and August Wentworth. Conrad Wentworth. Becky Wentworth-Jones. Paul Jones. Yes, WENTWORTH Wentworth. August is wearing a tie; Judith has on heels and one of her many elegant suits. Neither shows a hint of emotion. You have to know where to look if you want to gauge how they're feeling. Check the mother's hand. See how the tips of her nails are buried in the father's arm so deep that you can't even see her flawless French tip manicure? She's holding on for dear life. Looks like it would hurt, doesn't it?

Conrad, the eldest child, sighs and checks his watch. They've been waiting for over fifteen minutes. Five more and Conrad's going to have to start pulling some strings. Don't these people know who they're dealing with? Obviously not and if something doesn't happen soon . . . well, something better happen soon.

Becky wears an outfit almost identical to her mother's. Armani pant suit, gray instead of beige (he's one of their favorite designers). She stands next to her mother and from the back, you probably couldn't tell the two apart even though one is sixty-five and the other just thirty-nine. They have the same emaciated figure, the same perfectly straight hair, cut neatly at the chin. Becky is blond and while Judith has let some gray creep in you'd have to be standing pretty close to detect the difference in color. Judith and August are worried and a little scared, Becky is resentful. How dare she be called out in the middle of the night? She has a life of her own, you know. But Becky would be equally furious if they had left her out of this little crisis. She has an obsessive need to always be in the middle of things. Becky Wentworth-Jones, front and center. Drama is the wellspring of her life force.

Paul puts his arm around his wife but she stiffens and pulls away. The stress. Poor Becky is very susceptible to stress. It is an unfortunate situation but really, if she could just relax, everyone would feel better. Paul tries to rub her shoulders, release some of that tension.

"Knock it off, Paul." Becky adjusts her hair and smoothes her trousers.

Paul backs off. The sooner this whole thing is resolved, and he can get his wife home to bed, the better. Becky doesn't do well on too little sleep.

Here comes little brother Norman accompanied by a grim-faced policeman. At first glance you would swear that the Chanel suit he's wearing was his mother's except, of course, that he's much bigger than she is. He probably stole one of hers and had it knocked off—the parents keep him on a pretty tight leash and Norman doesn't have a lot of extra money to spend on clothes. He's carrying the pumps in his left hand—thank God. There are few things more unsettling than to see your son or baby brother walking around in high heels. One finds one doesn't know where to look when a young man like this is prancing around with his shaved legs stuffed in panty hose. The officer escorts Norman right up to the group then turns to go.

Judith stares. With the foundation and the artful highlights at the cheekbones, Norman could pass as her butch younger sister. It really is quite remarkable. Unfortunately, he hasn't completely wiped off his lipstick and there are red smears at the corners of his mouth. But his mascara is remarkably intact—must be waterproof. You've got to hand it to him; Norman knows his way around a make-up kit.

"Jesus fucking Christ." Conrad sticks his hands in his pockets and walks towards the exit then turns and rejoins the group. He finds it impossible to hold still in dicey situations like these. Hard to stand and be counted as part of a group like this—a family, his family—when one of the members is dressing up like Cinderella.

Becky takes her mother's hand and squeezes. Whether this is an act of support or a moment of need is unclear. Oh, the horror. Paul moves in to help but backs off when Becky bares her teeth.

August is working very hard to control his breathing.

Finally Judith says, "That's my good purse."

"I'm sorry." Norman starts unloading the purse. Careful Norm, don't want the parents to see that compact with your engraved initials. And uh-oh, are those a pair of lacy crotchless panties? Don't let Becky get a glimpse of those. Norman stuffs his belongings in the too-small pockets of the faux-Chanel jacket. One of the gold buttons is loose but now's not the time to worry about these things.

"Holy fucking shit." Conrad's off for another lap around the room.

Norman snaps the purse shut. "I borrowed these clothes from my friend Carol for the costume party but she didn't have a bag that matched." He thrusts the bag towards Judith, his peace offering.

"Costume party." August likes to restate the facts whenever possible. It grounds him, gives a nice sense of control. These family crises tend to knock August off balance.

"You know my friends Bill and Susan." Norman's picking up speed as if there's a time limit on this explanation. "This is just the

most ridiculous thing in the world." They all feel that clock tick-
ing. Norman rushes on. "It's an annual thing. I thought it would
be a hoot to dress as a woman." Change of tone here. "I'm so
embarrassed."

Now, Becky could point out that Bill and Susan live in Santa
Monica, which is on the other side of town. (It would be far too
cruel to announce that they are in fact in Europe until the 17th.)
She could ask him why he was in the bushes with another man in
the first place. But that's not her job here. Her job is to stand by
and act as a supportive witness to whatever story they come up
with. Marvelous fiction that will allow everyone to return to their
regular lives.

Judith is staring at her empty purse. "What will my friends
think?" she whispers to August then turns to Conrad, her eldest
and brightest child, for the answer.

"It's covered, Mother." Conrad clears his throat. "I've got people working on it right now. This whole thing will just go away.
Never happened."

"But what if it doesn't?" Judith's beginning to get angry.

August puts his arm around his wife and squeezes tight. No
one wants to see her explode. Her self-serving rage can fill a room
in an instant, making it extremely difficult to breathe. August will
have to hold onto her for the rest of the night to keep those nox-
ious tendencies in check. "No one is going to find out about this,
Judith."

"Mom, don't worry." Norman's attempt at being a man is seriously undermined by the pink lace bra strap that shows under his
opened jacket. "It's a trumped-up charge. Nothing to be concerned about."

Conrad leads the way and the family heads out into the night,
Judith roped in by August, Norman tiptoeing over pebbles and bits
of broken glass in the parking lot, and Becky and Paul bringing up
the rear. They all follow Conrad back to their cars. It's a quiet
group now—Norm hasn't really worked his magic yet. There are
huge holes in this story but it's three-fifteen, everybody's tired and

it's cold. Paul hasn't contributed much and he's starting to feel a little left out. This group needs to be united.

"Can you imagine what it must be like for those unfortunate transvestites," Paul says. "They get this kind of abuse all the time."

Bingo. Everyone jumps on this. Yes, those poor people. Wouldn't it be awful? What a terrible life. Norman, of course is the most vocal. August shakes his head at the injustice of the world. Becky pats her mother's shoulder then gives Norman a little hug. Judith is still angry. She'd like to punish Norman for this, and every other outrage he has committed over the years, but she's exhausted and so she plays along. Conrad doesn't contribute to the healing process but he doesn't interrupt either. And so the Wentworths come together here in the parking lot of the Los Feliz police station. They hug and kiss (except Conrad, who just shakes hands) and say good night. Judith and August climb into the back seat and sit staring out opposite windows while Norman slips behind the wheel of the Bentley. Becky climbs into her Jaguar and starts the engine as Paul gets in on the passenger side. Conrad speeds away. This will all be cleared up by morning, never to be spoken of again.

⎯

If you ask Norman where he lives, he'll tell you Bel Air. If you raise an eyebrow in appreciation of the neighborhood he'll tell you he has an adorable little cottage off Copa De Oro that's been in the family for years and years. Very New England, stone with a slate roof, built in the twenties. If you're interested, he'll go into great detail describing the climbing vines, the magnificent rose garden and the rock lined pool. Oh, it just sounds so wonderful and isn't Norman nice. But, if you try for an invitation to Norm's enchanted home, you'll notice he suddenly becomes distant and cool. He'd rather meet you at the bar on Santa Monica Boulevard or the coffee shop in Westwood or better yet, if you're a handsome young man, why not just meet at your place.

Poor Norman, he's embarrassed that at thirty-five he's still living in his parents' pool house and hasn't yet decided on a career. Yes, he has his own entrance off the alley so he can come and go as he pleases. Yes, the housekeeper does all his cleaning and laundry (with the exception of his lingerie and fem-wear which he keeps hidden and locked in the trunk under his bed.) Yes, his meals are free and, if he's nice to the staff, they're often served in his room. But with mother lurking around, looking in windows and often bursting through the door unannounced, he can hardly afford to entertain at home.

No, it's not an ideal situation for single young Norman but at this point there aren't a lot of options since his trust fund won't kick in until his parents decide he's ready. And so off they go, Mommy, Daddy and Normy, back to his childhood home and a good night's sleep while Becky and Paul drive home to their children and Conrad heads off to one of his after-hours club where he can blow off some steam.

The Wentworth Family—
A Proper Introduction

*W*hen at home, **AUGUST ELLIOT WENTWORTH** spends his time locked away in his vast yet comfortable office. His den. His lair. This is a place where he can be himself and shed the uncomfortable facade of family man, a place where August becomes "Gus." It is a masculine room with a wet bar, humidor and wild game—stuffed and displayed on the walls. Women-folk are not welcome here. There is a coffee table fashioned from antelope hooves that sits upon a zebra skin rug. A prized pair of elephant tusks is mounted behind the desk and four elephant's feet, severed just below the knee joint, serve as lamp stands and sit at the ends of the long ostrich skin sofas. Here and there are pictures of Gus on safari, gun in hand, triumphant smile on his face as yet another of God's creatures lays dying at his feet.

August is a big man, tall and wide with damp meaty hands and a thick neck. He tells people he played football in college, a lie in which his wife Judith firmly believes, but he does look like an aging athlete gone soft through the middle. He drinks and eats excessively and spends his time in an exhausting pursuit of pleasure. August loves women. He loves they way they smell, the way they taste. Nothing better than undressing a little cutie for the first time. Each one is different but they're all so warm and sweet, like little biscuits fresh out of the oven. Women make him feel like he's going to live forever, especially the young ones.

⎯

JUDITH WENTWORTH spends more time looking in the mirror than she does communicating with the world around her. She analyzes, she studies, she improves. Behold, Judith Wentworth, bone thin and chic in her Chanel suit and her perfect hair and make-up. Make no mistake about it, appearance is everything. Follow Judith down the street and watch her seek out the reflective surfaces of the storefronts and the car windows. Watch her pause and admire what God, and the plastic surgeon, have given her. Not a single line on that sixty-five-year-old face, no nasty sunspots to mar her perfect complexion. Judith Wentworth, size 2 American, 32 French, 36 Italian.

Judith (never Judy) has been married to August for forty-five years. Yes, it has been a successful marriage, not romantic, and perhaps not particularly warm, but solid. If you asked Judith about loyalty, she'll tell you it is the most important ingredient in a marriage. She'll assure you that August has been a good and faithful husband. There was a time, early in the marriage, before Judith had developed her ability to shape the world according to her own specifications, when August's extramarital activities invaded her every waking moment. His constant affairs almost killed her and, in fact, she did contemplate suicide. But that was years ago in another age and she has completely forgotten about it now. It simply never happened. She's married to a wonderful man and they share a wonderful life.

Conrad is the oldest of the three children and frankly the most attractive and successful. Judith and Conrad are very close. They talk on the phone daily and she confides in him. Judith trusts her oldest son in a way she's never trusted anyone. He is a very important lawyer with a good firm and a wonderfully attentive son.

Rebecca—Becky—is the middle child. She's not as bright as Conrad but is a sweet and devoted daughter. Rail-thin like her mother, the two women favor the same designers and often share clothes. Judith introduced Becky to her husband Paul. She encouraged her daughter to go forward with the wedding even though Becky was concerned that Paul might be a little boring, slightly dull. Judith pointed out that boring is very dependable. Paul is home for dinner every night. He drives carpool on Thursday. He's well groomed, a good provider and he's never once forgotten an anniversary or birthday. It is a good marriage for Becky.

Norman is the youngest of the three Wentworth siblings. He's Judith's special-needs child: gay, thirty-five and still living at home. When Norman was four years old Judith took him to the pediatrician to see if there was something they could do about that effeminate problem. Norman liked to parade around the house in Judith's high heels instead of playing outside with the other boys from the neighborhood. He would tuck his penis between his skinny little legs, stand pale and naked in front of the mirror and say, "Look Mommy, just like Barbie." Judith tries to think of him as retarded, deficient in a very fundamental way. He's never been able to hold a job. The poor boy can't seem to do anything. It helps her to remember that damaged goods cannot be held fully accountable for their actions. But she does wonder sometimes, late at night, if maybe she shouldn't have smoked during that pregnancy. Could smoking have caused her son to turn into a useless sissy? Is it her fault?

CONRAD WENTWORTH has a 2007 SLR McLaren. 5.5 liter, 36 valve V8, supercharged engine, 641 horsepower at 5000rpms. Thirteen miles per gallon city, seventeen highway. Black. With the extras, upwards of $500,000. That's right, five hundred thousand dollars. Don't touch it. Don't even breathe on it, understand? That's Conrad's car, step back. A little farther. Okay. It's clean, isn't it? Yeah, it is. Not a speck of dust on that sucker. Let's open the doors so you can look inside. Nice wood paneling, leather seats.

Can you smell it? He doesn't smoke or drink in his car, not even water. He knows about taking care of things.

Conrad is a real famous attorney and those things you might have heard about him; they're wrong, very unfair. Yes, he takes on the dirty cases, the stuff nobody else will touch, because Conrad Wentworth is not afraid. A music executive shoots a hooker in the face? Yeah, Conrad can help. A thirteen-year-old accuses some movie star of rape? Conrad can probably get him off. It's gonna cost, but that's what money's for. Money buys the best of the best and Conrad is it.

Pop the trunk. Yeah, that's a shotgun, semiautomatic. There's a .45 in the glove compartment and a little pistol under the driver's seat. Conrad's got a license to carry concealed weapons. The people he deals with—he needs to be armed. No big deal. See the stuff in the box, that's for his recreational activities. R & R. Tools of the trade. Guy like this, high-pressure job, needs to blow off a little steam. He's got to have something to help him unwind at the end of a long week and you know, golf just doesn't do it. So yeah, there's handcuffs and leg restraints, leather hoods with and without zippers, various sized butt plugs, bull whip, nipple clamps— your basic selection of playthings. Most of his gals like it rough and Conrad knows how to deliver. He's one popular guy.

—

I AM NORMAN WENTWORTH

A multidimensional being like myself can communicate with and understand the less evolved. But the two and even three-dimensional thinkers are utterly incapable of fathoming the depths to which my consciousness, my very soul, extends. Little minds work out little problems. The fluidity with which I conduct my day-to-day life is incomprehensible to the pea-brained members of my family and their ilk. Mine is a profound but wonderful journey.

Watch me now: I'm an astronaut. I'm the pool boy. I'm Genghis Kahn. I'm the French maid. I'm a rugby star. I'm Britney Spears. I'm an officer in the Navy. I'm Brigham Young with fifty-seven wives. I'm a leather queen. I'm Nancy Reagan. You see? Do you understand?

No. You're one of them, aren't you? I can see it in your eyes. You're one of the millions of Neanderthals, dragging your knuckles awkwardly across this earth, reacting with your dull and basic animal instincts. You could be a member of my family. You even look like them. Stupid and slow. Well, I recommend you stick to your own kind. Go on. Run away. Leave me alone.

Rebecca "Becky" Wentworth-Jones.

Conrad's the only one Daddy ever paid attention to. First born son and all that. They went hunting a lot. Hunting and fishing. Killing, that's what they had in common. But by the time I came along father was over the novelty of children and anyway what good is a daughter to a man like that? I don't really have many fond childhood memories of him. He was out of town a lot, safaris or hunting expeditions or off at his country club. Fine by me. Do you have any idea what it's like to be ten years old and have your father call you Fats? That's the nickname he gave me, Fats. He'd roll into town, look me over like I was some new and unidentified species of game, something he might want to shoot and stuff and put on his wall. He'd stare and then finally he'd recognize me and he'd yell, "FATS!" I wasn't really fat, just a little plump. I was ten. I'd yell, "My name is Rebecca." Mother would comfort me and say, "If you don't like it honey, lose it." Of course she was right, and I took care of the weight problem by giving up all carbohydrates at an early age but I've never forgiven my father. I never will.

Mother is my role model. Look at her, she's sixty-five and she's got the body of a thirty-year-old. She's so beautiful. She was really good about keeping me out of the sun. In summer when I was growing up and all my friends were at the beach, she'd keep me home and we'd go shopping or out to lunch. It was hard at the time because of course I wanted to be with kids my own age but as a result of her strict rules and discipline, I don't have any sun damage today. None. And all those kids I went to high school with, the ones who lay out and baked, well they look their age or ten years older and there is nothing they can do about it. Sun damage is irreversible, you know. I really owe my mom.

My husband Paul recently had a problem with his adenoids and the dangly bit in the back of his throat, the uvula. It was gross, that uvula, way too long and thick. Got to the point where I couldn't even look at him if he opened his mouth for fear of seeing that thing. Plus, he snored. I kept asking him to see a doctor, take care of the problem, but Paul's got a phobia about needles so he kept putting it off. The big baby. Finally I moved out of the bedroom and believe me, that got his attention. He had the surgery. They fixed the adenoids and cut out the uvula and now his throat is just a big open hole, nothing icky to look at, but since the surgery he's developed chronic halitosis and frankly I don't know what to do about it.

We've got two kids, Monica and Joey. I'm not a patient person and sometimes that's a problem, but Paul's a good father to them.

My brother Conrad is five years older so I didn't see much of him growing up. We're not close. He was off to college by the time I was twelve. Mother thinks Conrad's so wonderful, so impressive, but I think there's something weird about him. Have you heard him talk? He sounds like some sort of Italian mobster. He went East to school and came back with a tough-guy New Jersey accent. Perhaps he's compensating? And, I mean, why isn't he married? And why do all the women he dates look so much like mother? I think Mr. Oedipus might have a few words to say about the subject but my lips are sealed.

My little brother Norman is a fag. I'm sorry; I mean Norman is a homosexual. Norman likes to dress in women's clothes. He keeps all his costumes locked in a trunk under the bed. I don't really know why he bothers because we all know what's in the trunk but everybody plays along and pretends it doesn't exist. His tastes in clothing are very similar to mother's and mine. Sometimes he steals our things, purses and scarves. That's hard. But overall, I don't really care that he's gay. As long as he doesn't come around the kids wearing dresses, as long as he doesn't start singing the praises of sodomy, I'm okay. Paul has a hard time accepting it, but I'm okay.

—

PAUL JONES proposed to Becky with the intention of taking her name in matrimony, just as she would take his. He wanted them to be united, merged together as one, their names connected for eternity. But he wondered: would he be Paul Jones-Wentworth or Paul Wentworth-Jones? Becky loved the idea but she too was confused: Wentworth-Jones sounded better but was it the right choice? They went to Judith for help. Judith always had the answers. She was, after all, the one who introduced them. Well, Judith hit the roof. It was a stupid idea. Ridiculous. Who thought of it? Paul? Didn't he know that real men don't take their wife's name? He was born Paul Jones and he would stay Paul Jones. Period. Paul Jones. Paul wasn't sure, he'd heard of other men taking their wife's name, but Becky instantly agreed with her mother. And so he remained Paul Jones, husband of Rebecca Wentworth-Jones.

—

JOSEPH WENTWORTH-JONES is "Little Joey" to his parents, grandparents and everyone who knows him. If he thought about it, he'd probably prefer not to be called little since he is quite a fat boy and almost thirteen, but he doesn't think about it. Little Joey doesn't think about much of anything. He's a doer, not a thinker. He collects information and other people's things and stores them away where no one will ever find them. Look for him in the shadows. He blends in. And as long as he keeps his head down and his mouth shut, Little Joey's life is just fine.

—

MONICA JUDITH WENTWORTH-JONES
My mother Becky is a bitch and my father Paul wears a toupee. Oh, he doesn't know I know. He's never caught me spying

on him when he takes a shower but he's a full-on Friar Tuck, only his belly isn't so big. I spy on my bitch mother too but there's not much to report except that she looks like a bag of bones, she shaves all, ALL, of her pubic hair and she takes laxatives instead of vitamins. She's got scented candles burning in her bathroom twenty-four hours a day like some kind of voodoo shrine. God forbid anyone should smell her shit.

I've got nothing to say about Joey. He's just this lonely klepto. Hardly ever talks. Dull. You meet him and you think, something's wrong here. But he's my brother so, you know, somehow I feel responsible. The problem is, every time I'm in the same room with him, I want to break his fat neck.

Part One

1

August "Gus" Wentworth and His Girlfriend Honey

GUS SAT UP. IT WAS HOT. HONEY'S AIR CONDITIONER GROANED and sputtered in the window but it wasn't worth a damn. He'd have to buy her a new one if he was going to keep this up through the summer. Meat locker cold, that's how he liked his bedroom.

"Come here, Honey baby."

"I'm peeing."

Gus peeled himself off the sheets and walked to the bathroom.

Honey was seated on the toilet. She had her head down, concentrating, he supposed, on expelling all the urine in her bladder. The back of her neck was pale and flawless. Gus wanted to bite that neck. Everything about her was ripe. Honey's breasts were large and still very firm. You'd never guess she'd had a child. She had the narrow rear-end of an athlete which was a shock considering all the junk food she consumed. Cheese, fudge and fried food were the cornerstones in Honey's life. Gus didn't care. Twenty-one is twenty-one. It smells different. Sweet and fresh. Honey was perfect although if she kept eating the way she did she might not stay that way. You never knew how a person was going to age. Sometimes genetics are with you, but often they're your enemy.

Another couple of years, couple more kids, Honey might drop from the tree and spend the rest of her days rotting in the shade. But for the time being, her sun was definitely still shining.

"Don't look." Honey tried to push the door shut but Gus blocked it with his foot. "Can't I have a second of privacy Gus? Please."

Gus laughed. "Nope." Of course Gus was going to watch, that was what he came for. That's why he covered the rent for this little apartment. That's why he gave her the allowance and paid for the fancy daycare. He wanted to come over here and watch sweet Honey whenever he damn well pleased.

She finished peeing, wiped herself, flushed the toilet and hurried back into the bedroom without bothering to wash her hands.

Gus liked to shower at Honey's. Something about the stained porcelain tub, lack of water pressure, the cheap towels, gave the place an exotic feel. She was a terrible housekeeper—damp clothes on the floor, food containers in the trash, hair in the sink. Being in this apartment was a safari through the tangled jungle of the blue-collar worker, the great unwashed, the lower middle class. Gus liked it. He liked to use her Irish Spring soap and Suave shampoo, her floral scent antiperspirant and her French vanilla body lotion. He would arrive home smelling like a room deodorizer.

"Honey, come back in here." Gus pulled back the clear plastic shower curtain and turned on the faucet. He sat on the side of the tub and waited for the hot water. "Honey." The water turned hot. "HONEY."

"WHAT?" Honey had on her flesh-toned panties and matching bra. It tickled Gus that she didn't go in for sexy lingerie. She was plain, utterly basic and beautiful.

"Wash my back."

"I gotta pick up Kimmy at Happy Helpers."

"Please wash my back, Honey."

"I'm dressed."

"Honey."

Honey sighed then took off her underwear and stepped into

the tub with Gus. He handed her the soap and adjusted the water so it pounded hot on his stomach and crotch. Honey circled the soap round and round, starting at the small of his back and working upward. She worked fast, rushing her job, but Gus let it go. When the area was thoroughly coated she handed him the soap and went to work kneading and massaging his muscles. Gus taught her exactly how he liked his back washed on one of their first dates and now it was a part of every encounter.

"They get really mad if I'm late." Honey raked her nails up and down then pounded on his shoulders in an effort to wrap things up.

Gus soaped his penis and testicles. The cheap smell and the suds were extremely stimulating and he found himself aroused. He turned around and said, "Look what you did."

"I can't be late again," she said.

Gus put his soapy hands on Honey's breasts and circled the tight pink nipples. This little hayseed really did it for him. He closed his eyes and rubbed his soapy erect penis against her damp pubic hair.

"Kimmy cried last time," Honey said. "All the other kids had gone home."

Gus reached down and started fiddling around between her legs.

"I gotta go." Honey pulled back the shower curtain and was about to step out when Gus grabbed her arm.

"Please Honey. You are not through here." He tightened his grip and watched her face. He was awfully generous with her, she owed him. "You wouldn't leave me like this, would you?" He smiled and patted her shoulder. "It would be so cruel."

Honey dropped down onto her knees. The spray from the shower made it hard for her to breathe but somehow she managed. She sucked away and Gus closed his eyes. It felt so good. Honey's little pie hole. In and out, in and out. Not too hard, he didn't want to make her gag, but he took his time. Gus was in no hurry. He pumped her face until the hot water ran cold.

—

    Gus pulled his car into his garage and killed the engine. Twice in one afternoon, not bad for an old guy. This was the kind of news he'd like to share. "Hey Judith, guess what? I got it up two times today." "Judith, women like to fuck me. Young ones." "Judith, I'm sixty-seven. I'm a fucking stud." "Judith, I shot my wad all over a twenty-one-year-old's face." "Judith my dick still gets very, very hard." "Judith, you bitch, aren't you proud?" Gus got out of the car, adjusted his balls, and headed for the house.

2

What Norman Thinks

I am the son of a rutting philanderer. He's a man who likes hot pudding for breakfast, lunch and dinner. Judith does not provide that kind of nourishment and so he forages. To him, there is nothing more edifying than the sticky feel of feminine secretions on his worn and well-used baton. When he was young, my father could attract the finest of the species. August Wentworth was a master huntsman with astonishingly high levels of testosterone. Now that he's older, attracting female companionship has become more of a strategic business endeavor. It takes a little more work and the quality isn't always what it used to be. Still, he is the CEO, the CFO, manager and director, the monster cheese with biscuits, the ultimate liege lord of how to conquer and control women using excess money and a sprinkling of charm. His looks may have faded but a rich man like August can still usually take his pick.

You might ask: what about family values? Trust? Wouldn't the relentless pursuit of tail slacken the marital bonds? Mustn't it breed resentment in the poor, victimized spouse? And what about the offspring? Didn't that kind of behavior harm the sweet, vulnerable Wentworth children? Those loving and innocent youngsters, wouldn't they be confused by the lack of parental unity? My answer to you is that obviously they would be damaged. Children do not thrive when trapped in an environment of deceit. But I'm not one to dwell on the obvious. You must take those questions up with your own therapist, on your own time.

We as a species—yes I admit that you and I have that one thing in common, our place in the genetic cartogram—we human beings, are capable of adapting to endless configurations of adversity. A high pain threshold is crucial to survival. But three young Homosapiens, three Wentworth children, faced with the same hardships, will likely cope in very different ways. It all comes down to intelligence and natural selection. Survival of the fittest and the fittest is I.

And what of my reproductive future, you ask? You bemoan the fact I spill my seed fruitlessly? Then you obviously still believe in the virtue of perpetuating this human race. Well, I do not share your opinion, my friend. You and I are not of like mind.

3

Judith's Work is Never Done

Judith leaned over the porcelain sink to examine the single coarse black hair. It was long and black, obviously one of the maids, but which one? She reluctantly picked up the hair. Normally she wouldn't subject herself to such filth, she would call someone, but she had to personally get to the bottom of this. It was a long hair, at least to the shoulders, so that ruled out Graciela. Judith held it up to the light. It had the glossy sheen to it of the chemically untreated and the color was true black. Rosa. Had to be. Blanca colored her hair and Carmenita's was Negroid-kinky. Judith dropped the hair back into the sink and stepped out into the hall.

"Rosa." She used her calm but authoritative voice. One needed to assert one's position in a household full of help and Judith had perfected her leadership skills over the years. It was a terrible mistake to befriend these people. They didn't need a friend, they needed a boss. Judith was a master at setting limits and defining boundaries. Caring for the help was a lot like raising children except that the help never matured into adulthood. They were perpetual adolescents and required a firm hand. She waited thirty seconds, counting them off in her head, then called again, "Rosa.

Come down here, please." She counted. One one hundred, two one hundred. At fifteen she raised her voice. "Rosa, I want to see you this instant!"

"Coming, Missus," Rosa yelled from some distant room.

Judith looked around the bathroom. The linen hand towels were perfectly ironed and hung neatly on the towel rack. She reached over and creased the corner of one towel and crinkled another.

Rosa's heavy footsteps thundered down the front stairway. She arrived, panting, her mustache-prone upper lip dotted with beads of perspiration. Was it from fear or hard work? Rosa had been employed for over two years. Was she still so frightened of Judith? Judith smiled at the thought.

"I've been calling, Rosa."

"Yes, Missus?"

"I don't like to have to yell." Judith cleared her throat. "I expect you to come immediately."

"Sorry, Missus."

"Look here," Judith pointed toward the bathroom. "What do you see?"

"The powder room, Missus."

Judith nodded in encouragement. Sometimes these people could be so dense. Rosa looked reluctant to continue so Judith used her warm and supportive smile as a prod.

"The toilet," Rosa pointed. "The sink, the window, the soap, the hand towel..."

"Is this room clean?"

"Oh yes, very clean. I did it this morning."

"Step in here with me."

Rosa reluctantly stepped into the bathroom. Judith could smell the cheap floral soap and the underlying sweat. It must be the rice and beans that gave them that particular odor. Jalapeno peppers and lard.

"Children often have trouble concentrating on the task at hand," Judith said. She smoothed the front of cream-colored linen slacks. She would have to make this quick as she needed to change for dinner. "Follow through is an issue with the very young. You know that Rosa, you have children. Five children, correct?"

Rosa nodded her head. There were five children back home in Guatemala. Rosa sent money each week for food and clothing. She had not seen her children in three years and had no plans to return home anytime in the near future. She could not afford to leave.

"You and I, we are not children, Rosa." Judith pointed at the sink and the offending hair. "We are capable of better."

Rosa reached out to grab it but Judith caught her arm. "We can't really call this room clean, can we?"

Rosa shook her head. Was that a tear forming in her eye? Judith let the arm go and Rosa snatched up the hair and stuffed it into her uniform pocket.

"To me, stray hairs spell germs," Judith sighed. It was important that Rosa not forget this lesson. "Now, we expect to find hairs in public restrooms at football stadiums or gas stations or fast food restaurants but not in the home. Never in the home, Rosa. I can't live like this. With filth."

"It will not happen again, Missus."

"I hope not."

"Never."

"You promise me? Give me your word of honor?"

Rosa nodded. Yes, those were definitely tears in her eyes but Judith noticed that her hands were balled in tight fists.

"We'll let it go this time."

Rosa started to leave before she was dismissed. Silly girl was angry.

"Don't you have something to say, Rosa?"

Rosa turned like a defiant child. The fury in her eye made Judith want to laugh. These maids were from the third world, and yes their intelligence was not quite up to par, but they were not animals. They were capable of learning things. Didn't Rosa know that these lessons were for her own good? Didn't she understand that it was moments like this that would make her a better person?

Judith stared back until finally Rosa dropped her eyes.

"Thank you, Missus . . ."

"You're welcome, Rosa."

Rosa started to leave.

"Oh and Rosa? These linen hand towels need to be pressed with a very hot iron. You see? They're wrinkled. Do them again, please? I like everything to look nice when the family comes for dinner."

Rosa took the towels and hurried off and Judith continued her inspection of the house. She kept a running tally in her head of all the precious objects that she owned and all the things she intended to buy. Any *thing* that was lost or taken from her over the years went into a separate mental column, a special section labeled grudge or regret. Her calculations went back to childhood when she lived in a ratty trailer with a mother who had almost no money but an unlimited allowance for booze. But the conscious Judith of today had no memory of that ugly past. Her life was in order. The things that she owned, that she controlled, were comforting in a way that no human relationship could ever be. Her things were solid, and trustworthy; they had monetary value, heft and weight, and that made her feel whole. Judith Wentworth was safe.

4

Rosa

Rosa's jaw hurt from chewing the gum. She chewed and
sprayed the starch and chewed and ironed and chewed and folded
the linen hand towels. Snap, snap, snap went her teeth. It was a big
wad of gum, three pieces. The flavor was gone but Rosa kept on
working it. Missus didn't allow gum in the house. Rosa blew a bubble. Well, Missus could just come in here and take it out of Rosa's
mouth. Let her try. She'd lose a finger, that's what would happen.
Rosa would bite that skinny bitch's arm off.

There were a lot of rules in this house. This palace. No gum.
No colored nail polish. No hairspray. Those things were cheap.
Low class. And Missus was allergic. Missus could wear her own
perfume but Missus was allergic to everyone else's, so no perfume,
no scented lotions, no strong smelling soaps.

They were crazy, these people. Missus, with her perfect
things, starving herself all the time. And that horrible man, Mister
Wentworth, probably had two or three families scattered around
this city. Filthy dog. Can't keep it in his pants. Rosa knew lots of
men like him; she used to be married to one. No, she had no
patience with this type of person. One time Mister Wentworth put
that fat hand on Rosa's back end when she passed him in the hall.

Rosa turned around and scratched him with her nails. She drew blood. No man could get away with that. Never again. Rosa scratched him then she let out a scream that could have raised her dead grandmother but instead brought the Missus running.

Missus yelled, "What on earth is going on?"

Mister Wentworth tried to cover his arm. "Everything's fine."

"Oh my God," Rosa cried. She pulled his arm out for everyone to see. "You're bleeding! Look, Missus. Blood is dripping down."

And sure enough, there were three long scratch marks on his arm, all oozing bright red blood.

"August," Missus said. "How did this happen?"

He said some ridiculous story about nails in the garage and falling off a ladder. Not convincing but the Missus, she bought it. She never once asked why Rosa had screamed, never even looked at Rosa. Absolutely no questions were asked. Some women are like that; they don't want to see the truth about their men. Rosa was once like that herself until the day her husband ran off and left her with five young children and no money.

"That could get very infected, Mister Wentworth," Rosa said as she looked him in the eye. "A very, very big problem for you."

Missus took him by the hand and rushed him off to get a Band-Aid. Mister Wentworth never bothered Rosa again. She would take what she had to from Missus, she needed the money, her children needed the money, but no man would ever take advantage of Rosa Alvarado again.

Rosa stuffed another piece of gum in her mouth. Four pieces was a little much but she liked the sugary taste of strawberry. Something about the artificial flavor, a flavor that had nothing to do with real fruit, was soothing.

She had been working in the Wentworth house for two years. Two years and the older children, Conrad and Becky, still hadn't bothered to learn her name. They called her "the short one" or "the little Mexican girl." Rosa didn't care. Why should she? It was all about money. It was about her children, the only people she loved, the only reason she could think of to keep on living this miserable life.

Norman made a point of asking about the children and even remembered their names. He was all right. Crazy, no question, but nice. Who cares if he dressed up in his mama's clothes and pranced around like a fairy? He was the only decent person in this family and he didn't really belong.

Rosa finished the towels, turned off the iron, took the fat wad of gum from her mouth, rolled it around in her fingers to make a nice big wet ball then stuck it to the bottom of the sorting table next to all the other pieces she'd put there. It was a good collection. She made a point of buying different colored gums for variety. Soon the underside of the table would be completely covered with old chewing gum but there was still a chair and of course the ironing board. Rosa envisioned a world in which the bottom of every table and chair, counter and sofa in the Wentworth home, would be covered with her furiously chewed bubble gum. It would take a long time, but that Rosa had. Time. She would work for the rest of her life to give her children a better chance than she had. This house was her children's future. She had to keep this job and smile no matter how bad she felt. No tears allowed in the Wentworth house, no homesickness. She was a servant and only as good as her job. Rosa picked up the re-ironed hand towels and took them back downstairs to the powder room.

5

Norman's World

Judith would say: Charming English cottage, leaded windows, stonewalls and a heavy wooden door hewed from an ancient redwood. The Cotswold's, moss and ivy and smoke trailing lazily from the chimney. A meandering path with a sweet little bridge that crosses the babbling brook. Towering pine trees, cool and restful shade even on the hottest days. Silence and peace. Yes, it cost a fortune but it was worth every penny. You'd never guess that this was Bel Air, California. Not twenty-first century, more like seventeenth.

Norman would say: Hansel and Gretel with a huge pot of boiling water hanging over an open fire. The wolf's mouth, wet with blood and gristle. Ten thousand witches cackling in the gloom of an evil forest. Toadstools and poison apples. Little Red Riding Hood on her way to grandma's house and no kind woodsman in sight. An impossible tangle of thorny branches that barred his escape.

This was not what Norman had pictured for himself at age thirty-five. There should have been some trendy condo in West Hollywood. A townhouse with contemporary furniture and scores of beautiful young men. Models and actors of all races, everyone with a big personality and riotous sense of humor. These should have been his friends. Norman's phone should ring off the hook. They'd all go out on Friday or Saturday or even

Sunday night to Circus Disco or Fubar or Rage and party till the sun came up. Norman would have them all back to his place where he'd make eggs and bacon and they'd all slug down Bloody Marys in a preemptive strike on that inevitable hangover.

There should be a job that he had to go to on Monday morning, something smart and stylish. Fashion or advertising or maybe magazine work. Norman had the potential to be brilliant in any number of professions. His colleagues would love him. They knew he was meant for greatness.

But Norman didn't live in a condo, and Norman didn't really have any friends, and there had never really been a job. He lived here, in the guesthouse of his parents' mansion. He was stuck in this backyard fantasy of his mother's world. He was the project that gave Judith a sense of purpose. Taking care of poor Norman made her feel charitable and good. The constant nagging filled her time and allowed her never to examine her own existence. Norman provided her with the alibi that allowed her to believe that they were all living happily ever after.

Norman had tried to leave countless times, but the outside world sent him running back. It was just so damn hard to concentrate out there. So many things tugged at him. It took all his strength to keep track of the pieces. The struggle to remain whole, to keep his soul intact, required every ounce of strength that Norman had. He knew it wasn't like this for everyone. Other people functioned just fine. Even the imbecilic members of his family managed to live in the real world. Norman knew that some key part had been left out of his constitution. Someone had fallen asleep on the assembly line just as Norman slid by. They forgot to include the tiny engine that would power him up those steep mountains and now it was too late to start again. And so Norman lived here, locked away in this dark room at the back of his parents' house, surviving on anger and delusions and any kind of drug he could get his hands on.

Norman lay back on the bed and closed his eyes. He could feel the chemicals mixing with his blood. He waited. So relaxed. This was where he belonged, here in his bed, away from the world. And suddenly he was in Egypt with the Pharaohs and the Sphinx. They were waving. Hello, old friends. Magically, Norman was flying through the Valley of the Kings. He felt welcome here. Ramses II called out his name as he went by. Swish. The majestic pyramids were beautiful in the afternoon light. And here came Cleopatra with her shiny black hair and snaky bracelets.

"Hello, Cleopatra," said Norman.

She approached, whispered in his ear and offered him some feta cheese.

"No thank you, Cleopatra," Norman said. He flew on.

Tutankhamen was there. He had a very nice beard, not like the punky little goatees you see today on every street corner but a nice thick pelt spilling down his chest. It was regal and manly. The stuff of kings. And remarkably he showed absolutely no body hair. What a handsome man! His skin was taught and tanned and flawless, the kind of body Norman dreamed about. Norman was about to invite Tutankhamen to join him on the bed when the phone rang.

Norman lay perfectly still.

Ringggg.

Norman clasped his hands over his ears.

Ringgggg.

"No. No. No." Norman curled into a ball.

Ringgggg.

"Stop." Norman squeezed his eyes tight in an effort to hold onto his Egyptian friends but the constant ringing banished them from the room. He rolled over and covered his head with a pillow. If only he could make the noise go away. But the answering machine picked up and he heard the voice that was always there, tearing at him, pulling him down into her special kind of hell.

"Norman. Honey. Pick up."

Norman played dead and lay very still.

"Norman. Pick up now. I mean it."

Norman held his breath.

"Norman!" Judith's voice was battery acid in his eyes. "There's a lot to do before everyone arrives and I need you to come light the candles and start the fire in the living room."

Norman opened one eye and checked the machine. He had to make sure that Judith wasn't somehow using the device as an entry to his room.

"Norman." She screeched into the machine, "NORMAN."

She couldn't hurt him. Not in his room. He wouldn't let her.

"I'm going to count. If you don't pick up this instant I'm coming out there. One. Two . . ."

Norman sat up. He couldn't allow her toxic aura to invade his tranquil lair. This was his place in the universe, his domain, and no one was allowed inside. The single small room and attached bathroom, this "guesthouse," was the source of all his power and he must protect the integrity of his sacred space. His life depended upon it. Norman switched gears and picked up the phone.

"Sorry, Mother. I was in the shower."

"I need you."

"Coming."

"Slacks," Judith said. "Wear the slacks that Rosa left outside your door. You look so nice in those and Conrad's bringing a date."

Norman walked to the mirror and gazed upon his naked self. Could he grow a beard like Tutankhamen's? Yes, of course he could. Anything was possible. He opened his closet and took out his leather-riding chaps. How would mother like these? Just the chaps and nothing else? What would she say if he came to the dinner with his prized possession highlighted in such a creative and unusual way?

"My, Norman. You have a beautiful penis. No wonder you're so popular with all the boys. August, look at Norman's lovely penis. Too bad Conrad didn't get one like that. Turn around Norman. Let me look at your bottom." And Norman would turn and the family would all agree that his was the nicest ass on the face of this particular planet. But no. Not tonight. Not ever.

6

At Home with the Wentworth-Joneses

Rebecca "Becky" Wentworth-Jones stomped up the stairs to Monica's bedroom. Paul and Little Joey were all dressed and ready, waiting patiently downstairs on the sofa. Little Joey didn't mind getting dressed up for the grandparents. Little Joey wore whatever his mother told him to wear: khaki slacks, white button down shirt, navy blue blazer, just like his daddy. Sweet Little Joey. He was a good son, loving, obedient, and delightfully malleable. He accepted that the parents knew better. Why couldn't Monica be more like her brother?

Monica's door was closed. Her door was always closed. Closed and bolted with the music blasting away and tendrils of incense smoke sneaking out from the crack at the bottom. Becky wasn't sure what her daughter was smoking behind that barricaded door but she was certain that the incense was not there to enhance her yoga experience.

She knocked. "Monica, everyone's waiting for you." Becky smoothed the front of her skirt. She and mother had bought identical skirts in different colors with the agreement that they would swap every few weeks. It was so nice to wear the same size as one's mother; sharing clothes was such a bonding experience. Monica had already reached a whopping size eight by the time she got to junior high so Becky had never had the experience of sharing with her daughter. Not that Monica would ever be interested in anything Becky had.

"Monica. You need to come out now. I refuse to be late again because of you. It's rude and just because you don't care about rude doesn't mean that the rest of us have to be brought down by your bad manners. It upsets me. It upsets your grandmother. It upsets your father. It simply is not fair."

Monica stood behind the door and listened. Once her mother flipped the switch it was virtually impossible for her to shut it off. She could stand there and rant until the Botox wore off and the frown lines reappeared between her brows. Rain or shine, from morning to night, Becky felt compelled to badger and harp. It was her life's work, her destiny. Poor Becky. Hers was not a complex mind, more like the electricity experiment Little Joey did for his science project in the fifth grade. Touch the two wires together and watch the dim bulb burn.

"Coming, Becky," Monica said.

"You're not allowed to call me that." Becky pounded the door for emphasis. "You know you're not allowed to call me that. Mother. Mom. Mommy. Those are acceptable names. Not Becky. Never Becky." She pounded again. "Open this. Right now."

It was like teasing a puppy with a sirloin steak and a long sharp stick, cruel but enormously entertaining. "One second, MOMMY."

"You listen to me, Monica Judith Wentworth-Jones. When I say jump, you say 'How high?' and I say open this immediately or I'll call your father."

Monica checked her nose for coke. Becky, and just about everyone related to her, excluding Monica of course, had the brain capacity of a single cell amoeba but she did have weird narc-like instincts that forced Monica to take extra precautions.

"Paul," Becky yelled. "Paul, we need to break down Monica's door. She won't come out. PAUL. Come up here. Monica won't open. We've got a real problem."

Monica gently tore open one end of a super sized tampon, slid the little vial of coke inside the cardboard applicator then closed the wrapper and buried the tampon in the bottom of her purse.

"**PAUL!** I need some help here. Come. Now."

Monica took one more deep sniff, hoping to suck in some un-utilized nugget of cocaine that might be lying dormant in her nasal cavities, then opened the door and stepped out into the hallway just as Becky was heading down the stairs to marshal her forces for an all-out attack. "Here I am, Mommy. Off we go to Grandmother's house."

7

The Secret World of Little Joey

Joey sat in the back seat behind his father, Monica behind her mother. Girls' side, boys' side. Paul drove, Becky fumed, Monica was all squirmy, and Joey worked the hangnail on his right index finger with his teeth. They all stared out the windows. No one spoke. What Joey would have liked to do is take his finger down a couple more layers, just to where it started to ooze, but he had to be careful. Bleeding made Becky angry. She'd say, "Paul, make him stop. Why does he do that? Do we need to take him to a doctor? Joey, is something wrong with you? What's wrong with you, Joey?"

No. Joey didn't want that kind of attention. Joey just wanted to be left alone with his thoughts and his plans. So he sat quietly and watched the world go by and made do with the gentle nibbling of his fingers and his thumbs.

Gnawing animals, or rodents, are a varied group. Some are cute, even cuddly. Beavers, for instance, with their fat bodies, stubby legs and big flat paddle tails, are adorable. Those darling beaver teeth can saw right through an entire stand of trees in no time flat.

A beaver is an industrious animal, always building nifty little dams and swimming to and fro. Everyone loves a busy beaver. Squirrels are very popular too, their cheeks full of nuts, their dens all cozy and snug. Squirrels often store large supplies of food in the ground or in stockpiles near their nests. They defend their territory with surprising ferocity yet they are charming and sweet when not engaged in warfare. And, like elephants, squirrels have a good memory and a keen sense of smell, which helps them find and retrieve their hidden treasure during the winter months. You find sweet little beavers and fluffy squirrels starring in children's tales throughout the world. They are beloved animals and by far the most popular of the gnawing animals.

If you asked Little Joey which animal in the rodent family he most resembled, he would no doubt pledge allegiance to the squirrel and the beaver. He would cite his tendency to hoard supplies and compare it with that of the squirrel who spends his year on an obsessive survival quest to prepare for winter. Little Joey would say that his ability to construct hiding places for his belongings was much like the beaver's dam building skills. He considered himself a master craftsman, clever and determined. He had his treasures secreted throughout the house and no one suspected a thing.

It was true that Little Joey did in many ways resemble both of these animals but not in ways he would like to acknowledge. His fat body and squat legs were indeed beaver-like and the still protruding front teeth and beady eyes were very much like those of the common ground squirrel. But Little Joey was neither adorable nor charming and, truth be told, it was the rat family which could claim the most direct kinship.

Pack rats, or woodrats as they are more commonly called, are obsessive thieves. They are nosy creatures and curious about everything that goes on around them. They covet other people's belongings and hide or carry home small articles that catch their fancy such as silverware, nail clippers, buckles, tin foil, paper clips, jewelry, brightly colored stones and even manure. The pack rat doesn't have any use for these stolen wares but will obsessively hide and guard them. It is the feeling of ownership that gives this rodent its sense of purpose and the quest for loot that drives each waking hour of a pack rat's life. So too with Little Joey Wentworth-Jones.

Little Joey started stealing the moment he could effectively use his hands. If he could grasp it, he could own it. If it belonged to someone else, he wanted it. He stuffed things in his diaper— spoons, ashtrays, books of matches, only to be punished later when the befouled diaper needed to be changed. Little Joey understood that stealing was dangerous and carried with it the potential for great consequence and so from a very young age he developed uncanny abilities in the area of stealth behavior. He stopped using his diapers as a hiding place and began his life work of seeking out the dark and forgotten places where he could safely store that which was rightfully his.

Monica was the biggest potential problem in Little Joey's life. She caught on to him early and knew exactly what he was up to. When he was five years old, Monica saw him steal Becky's earring and hide it in the small space between the freezer and the wall of the pantry.

"Paul, Paul!" Becky shouted later that evening after a few too many glasses of wine. "I've lost my good diamond earring." She got frantic whenever she lost something. "Children, help me find it. LOOK! Now."

Monica didn't tell. She followed Little Joey around, pretending to hunt for the earring. When they were "searching" the library and out of ear shot from the parents she whispered, "You little shit. I'll kill you if I ever find you in my room."

"Okay." Joey pretended to look amongst the cushions on the couch. He dared not make eye contact with his sister.

"Don't you ever touch any of my stuff." Monica kicked him hard on the left shin. "Understand?"

Little Joey grabbed his shin and fell to the ground in pain but he didn't make a noise. He lay on the floor, fighting back the tears, as his sister left the library and headed back towards the living room where her parents were tearing the furniture apart. He heard her say, "Did you find your earring yet, Mommy?"

The key to not getting caught was not being noticed. Little Joey found that if he did exactly what his mother asked of him, and if he did it quietly, she would pay him very little attention and he would remain free to plunder.

If you asked Little Joey why he stole, why he felt the need to hoard other people's stuff, he would just shrug. Little Joey wouldn't be able to tell you that taking things was his way of controlling the world.

8

Conrad on Angela Simms

*A*ngela Simms is the stupidest bitch I ever fucked. Stupid but perpetually in heat. She's got a pussy that is always wet. She keeps it waxed and smooth just the way I like it. I can't get enough of that, know what I'm saying? You might think she's a little skinny, but I like that little girl look. Fat chicks should be killed.

"Oh my God," Angela says. "Conrad, it's the size of the White House."

We're at my parents' house for dinner. This is her big *meet the family* night.

"God, I hope they like me." Angela is flipping open that mirror on the sun visor for the seventy-eighth time.

"Honey, stop with the mirror," I tell her. She's driving me crazy with that shit. She's wasting her time, anyway. Doesn't matter what she looks like or how much preparation she goes through, they're not going to like her. They don't like anyone. I reach across the seat and pat her knee. "You're perfect, honey. They'll love you."

The thing about Angela, the thing that has kept me coming back long past the expiration date, is this crazy sex thing. I can send her into a fucking frenzy without hardly trying. This is the horniest bitch that ever walked the planet. Watch this:

I lean over and kiss her. At first she pulls back, afraid to mess her lipstick cause she's real nervous about tonight. But I grab the back of her head and force her—real rough. She loves rough. Then I suck on her tongue the way she likes it, kind of like a calf pulling on a teat. I lick her teeth and slide my hand along her left thigh. Hear that moan? I've been at it for what? Twelve seconds? She's like a novelty act in the circus. I've never seen anything like it. I mean I can just say the word *pussy*, and she gets all squishy. One little word and she's ready to go. And she'll do anything I tell her. Gangbang, bondage, blindfold, electrical currents—it's all the same to Angela. All sex is good sex.

Now watch this: I move my hand up between her legs, pull her panties to one side and work that magic little button with my index and middle finger. She likes this little twisting motion—real fast. See? She's riding my hand, immediately and completely oblivious to the fact that we're parked in my parents' driveway and already twenty minutes late for dinner. Anybody could walk outside and see this. Crazy, huh? Okay, her checks are all red now, that's the sign that she's all fired up. So, now I remove my hand and sit back. We can just enjoy the show from here on out, she'll take care of the rest.

The thing about Angela is that once I get her started she can't stop. It's like a survival thing: when aroused, she must achieve orgasm or die. Doesn't matter where we are, if I can get her going—and I always can—she's going to finish the deal. I've pulled this at the supermarket, department store, restaurants, even at the preschool where she works. It's really a trip. Look how she's got her legs spread wide. She's a bit of an exhibitionist with me, but hey, it's a pretty nice view don't you think? See how she's replaced my hand with hers. Here comes the audio part of our show:

"Oh. Oh, oh, oh. Ohhhhhh."

Yeah, she's not that creative with the dialogue, but still, it's fun to watch. Should I roll down the windows and let the world enjoy the mating cries of Angela Simms? What would Judith think?

Actually, if Judith happened to wander outside, we could probably forget about the dinner.

"You make me so wet, Conrad. Ohhh. Awwww."

See how Angela's using both hands now? She really gives that thing a workout. I'm going to turn on the interior lights. If Judith did happen to walk outside, we want to make sure she has a good view of what's going on. Oops, Angela stops, confused by the light.

"Don't stop, baby," I say. "I need to see you. You make me hard, Angela. Very hard."

See? That's all it takes. She's back to work with renewed enthusiasm.

"In my mouth, Conrad," she says. "Please."

"Yes, baby in your mouth." I say. "I'll bash out those teeth."

"My hair," she says. "Do it all over my face."

See how she's yelling now? These fantasies of hers seem to be more powerful when the decible level rises. Crazy wench.

"Oh no. You put it in my BUTT," she cries. "It's in my butt."

"Yes," I say. "Yes honey, it's in your tight little butt and I'm going to bust you wide open."

"Ouch. Ouch, oh ouch."

I gotta roll down the windows. This is too fucking good. I need to share it with the whole family. Look at her, the fucking car is shaking. She is driving those hips so hard.

"It hurts, it hurts, it hurts it hurts."

See? That's the thing. She likes pain. 'Cause seriously, orgasms don't hurt but she always says ouch. I dig that. Something about hurting a woman really turns me on. I'm actually getting pretty hard talking about this. You?

"Make it stop. Stop. STOP."

Okay, she's done now. It always ends with a big *STOP!* She'll sit there quietly for a while. Looks like she just ran a marathon, doesn't it? It'll be a couple of minutes before she realizes where we are and what's just happened. It's like she's had some kind of seizure—an X-rated epileptic fit—and she often doesn't completely remember what she did. Only difference is, she doesn't foam at the mouth. Pretty fucking wild, huh? Watch this:

"Baby, give me your panties."

She got those things off fast, huh? I take a big sniff. Women love it when you make of show of loving their stink.

"I'm gonna keep these, sweetie. Every time you see my hand in my pocket I'm playing with your panties."

"Oh Conrad, you're making me hot again."

"I'm gonna rub the crotch and you're gonna feel it all the way across the table."

She's reaching down there to start all over again but you've seen enough.

"Sweetie, you keep your eyes on me all night." I lean in and give her a kiss. "I'm gonna make you cum all over my mother's velvet chair."

She's swooning but it's time to get this show on the road. I climb out of the car and walk around to open her door. This is her farewell dinner. She doesn't know it, but we're at the end of the line. As good as she just was, it's getting old. I'm giving her dinner with the folks and then *adios* Angela Simms.

9

Family Dinner
(Norman's Not Hungry)

Norman was a robin's egg, all fragile and baby blue. His shell was thin and vulnerable but his yolk, which floated gently inside, was firm, plump and yellow. And there he sat in a room full of egg sucking predators. They had long sticky tongues and waddled vulture's necks. Sharp talons. The sap of their dishonest lives oozed from their eyes and noses and gaping pores. Mouths opened and closed. Razor teeth. They were taking up too much space, these people, with their dinner plates and salad plates and bread plates and knives and forks and glasses. Laughing. Yes, they would like to break his beautiful delicate shell. They would drop him out of his nest and watch him smash on the ground far below then walk away without a second glance. Norman closed his eyes.

Judith was telling the story about the magazine people who wanted to photograph the house. She said, "You know, we simply don't associate with people like that. Can you imagine?"

Everyone nodded in agreement as August walked around the table and poured the wine.

Conrad said, "Mother, Angela thinks this is a beautiful house, don't you Angela?"

Angela nodded, enthusiastically. Judith thought she was a pretty girl. Beautiful, in fact. Conrad certainly had good taste in women.

———

Becky watched Angela lick her lips and run her hand along her throat, down towards her chest. God. It always came down to sex with Conrad. Why couldn't anyone else in the family see how sick he was? Look how she squirms in her seat. She'd do anything for him, just like all the others. Girl after girl, year after year. How did he find them? Conrad only went for the one model—Judith Wentworth circa 1969. His women were identical down to the thin upper lip, sharp chin and the long fingers and nails. He always brought them at the end of the relationship, just before he dumped them; no girl was ever invited twice. It made Becky sick. Conrad was the overindulged house cat who didn't hunt out of need but for sport and when he was victorious he instinctually brought home his trophy to Master Judith and proudly displayed the bloody carcass, feathers and all. The strange thing was that instead of being repulsed by this twisted ritual, Judith seemed to enjoy it. She liked meeting these pathetic women. Becky took a sip of water. Goddamn it. It just wasn't fair.

———

August took his seat and raised his glass. This was the signal for them to focus on the wine. Very serious. Concentrate. Hard. August swirled the wine, scrutinized the color, vacuumed the bouquet with his slightly red nose. Finally he put the glass to his lips and pulled the wine into his mouth as if he were sucking marrow from the bone of a freshly killed animal. He savored the flavor, swallowed then nodded and everyone grabbed their glasses and drank.

"Baked apple, a little caramel." August cleared his throat. "It thoroughly bastes its spice and mineral flavors in butter."

Paul nodded enthusiastically. Usually they went around the table counterclockwise which meant Paul would have gone last but tonight he felt confident in what he had to say and so he jumped in even though, technically, it wasn't his turn. To be honest, Paul had a hard time with the wine talk. He couldn't tell the difference between cassis and chocolate, tropical fruit and tar. But tonight a light went off when the wine hit his palette. Tonight he was pretty sure he had it right. Paul cleared his throat, sat up tall and said, "I taste lots of minerals, August. It's velvety and lush. Rich and dare I say, a little sexy?"

Monica watched Paul. He spent his life trying to win her grandfather's approval, as if August was the wizard who was handing out the brains, but it was a waste of time because, unbeknownst to Paul, the wicked witches at the far end of the table had his balls locked up in the freezer. They were saving them for some evil feast and no one could stop them. The demon power of Judith and Becky was far too strong for a simpleton like Paul. He was just too weak and, Monica suspected, maybe even a little gay. August couldn't save him. No one could. Poor Paul was doomed and at that moment Monica almost felt sorry for her father, but not quite.

Judith ignored Paul as usual. She couldn't stand to have control of the evening slip away, even for a second. Paul should have waited his turn. Judith cleared her throat and said, "Pear. Does anyone get pear? Pear pulp? Monica?"

Norman drained his glass and refilled. He considered slipping away for a big snort of Ketamine or perhaps a few more puffs of hash. Maybe he could bring back some rat poison for his mother.

———

Angela Simms dutifully drank her wine. Would she have to perform those silly sex acts for Conrad once they were married? Would she have to be his nasty little porn star for the rest of her life? His screaming nymphomaniac? No way. Wives didn't have to do that shit. Girlfriends did it to sink the hook but once you got that marriage certificate, it was all over. Hell, she probably wouldn't even have to give him a blowjob once she was Mrs. Conrad Wentworth. Angela looked around the table. No way did Judith Wentworth suck on that old man's dick. And Angela couldn't imagine Becky servicing anyone but herself. Marital bliss was a license to shut it all down. Angela was tired of fake orgasms and constant moaning. She was tired of pretending to be turned on by every little thing Conrad said. Idiot. Did he really think he was that hot? She took another sip of wine. Men were so stupid.

———

It was Monica's turn. The Wentworths were adamantly opposed to drugs but somehow didn't mind about children drinking wine. Monica suspected her grandmother was behind this and that it had something to do with imaginary European roots.

Monica said, "Yeah, I got pear Grandma. But I'd say it has a fruit forward personality with a hint of quartz and although friendly, it's certainly not shallow. I wouldn't single out pear."

———

"Very good, Monica." August clapped his hands then reached over and caressed Monica's cheek. "Excellent." She was such a pretty girl and very smart. Monica tried to pull away but August held her chin and looked into her eyes. What kind of woman would she become? What kind of man will she choose? She had her whole life ahead of her. So many options.

———

Norman pushed his chair back from the table. Didn't anyone notice that Grandpa was drooling? Didn't anyone care? This was too much, he needed to go. Bring in Caligula. Disembowel the visitor. Let August rape his granddaughter while Conrad finally consummates the mother-son relationship he's longed for all his life and Paul can sodomize his kleptomaniac son. Let them wallow in their incestuous filth. Let them destroy each other and burn in their self-made hell. He was leaving. Norman stood.

Judith said, "What do you think you're doing Norman?"

"Just going to lie down for a minute. I think I have a fever."

"Sit." Judith's voice was like a bullwhip lashing his delicate and sensitive mind. The sting of her command took his breath away and with it his power. Norman found himself dazed and momentarily paralyzed. He gently lowered himself back down on the chair.

———

Conrad brought his fingers to his nose. He looked Angela in the eye and took a long sniff. Truth was, he couldn't smell anything, but he closed his eyes and rocked his head back. Oh baby. He opened his eyes and gave her that look. Yeah. She was getting hot. He made her hot. Look at her squirm. He would almost be sorry to see her go.

———

Angela knew that landing Conrad was not going to be a picnic. She knew that bringing her home to the family was probably his farewell gift. She fully expected him to serve her with the walking papers—as early as tomorrow. He probably looked forward to it; guys like this love to break women's hearts. Well, bring it on. Conrad Wentworth had no idea what he was dealing with.

Angela was ready for whatever he could throw at her because she and the future Conrad Jr. (or perhaps Connie?) had a much better set of plans.

———

Judith turned her attention to Little Joey who was sucking on a butter knife. "Little Joey, tell your grandfather. What do you think of the wine?"

Little Joey was thinking about what was in Angela Simms' purse. He was working on a plan. Two minutes, that's all he'd need. He put the knife back on the bread plate and addressed his grandfather. "Toast?" He took a deep breath. "And maybe raspberries with a little apple?"

———

August shook his head and laughed. "Where in the world did you get toast?"

Little Joey examined his hands.

August looked around this table at his family. They shared his blood. Three generations enjoying yet another meal, together. August felt proud. He looked at his grandson. Couldn't really see a resemblance but maybe, as the boy got older.

"Try again, Joey," August said. "Clear your mouth with water first."

Little Joey had some water then took another sip of the wine. "Honeydew melon?"

"Yes," August said. "Very good, Joey. It's subtle, you really have to look for it but I definitely get honeydew melon." August reached over and patted the boy on the head.

"I got a cold." Little Joey said. "Couldn't taste right the first time."

August smiled and then raised his fork and knife. This was the traditional Wentworth signal to begin.

10

Norman Goes Back to His Room

*E*xocannibalism: members of a group or tribe kill and then eat people from other tribes. Eating the body and brain of an enemy will make you stronger and provide you with great magical powers.

Endocannibalism: members of a group or tribe that eat their own, usually after they've died of natural causes. This is a way to honor the ones you love and to keep them with you forever. The practice is often referred to as "Mortuary Cannibalism," and is considered the most compassionate way of devouring one's fellow man.

Then there is the very pedestrian Survival Cannibalism, which in Norman's mind didn't even count. Cannibalism should involve conscious decision in the face of other options. One must choose to eat another person even when faced with an abundance of other dining options. Fingers and toes instead of hooves or claws.

Deviant cannibals are what Norman called the crazies: the impotent guy who killed women then ate their genitals (hair and all?). The gay guy who drilled holes in his victim's skulls, thus rendering them zombies, then raped and finally ate them.

These guys weren't proper cannibals. They didn't run with a tribe. They weren't warriors and Norman had no interest in them.

If Norman killed and ate his family would he be an exocannibal or an endocannibal? There was no question that they were the enemy. Judith and August were the king and queen of psychological punishment, the masters of intellectual enslavement, heroes of repression and dimwitted dogma. Oh yes, Judith and August and all their offspring were his evil foe and should be destroyed. But there was no denying the fact that Norman was one of them. He shared their blood. He was the fruit of those wretched loins. So would it be exo or endo?

There would be a fire and a spit made from jungle logs. He'd have his family tied in groups of two. Judith and Becky. August and Conrad. Monica could have her own log. Little Joey would be left at home.

"Help, help," they'd scream.

He'd lift them onto the spit and roast them slowly over that raging flame. Norman would delight in their screams and horror.

"You see?" he'd say. "You see what you get?"

Drums would keep a constant beat and he would dance around the flames, as they died their slow and torturous death. And when they were perfectly cooked he'd tear their flesh off with his hands, scoop out the eyeballs, crack the skull and gorge himself. Eat and eat until his stomach was close to bursting and his face and body were greasy with their succulent juices. Then later he would defecate, huge piles of shit. Family shit. And he'd leave those piles there on the ground in the jungle clearing as a monument to what they'd done.

11

Who is Paul?

$\mathcal{P}$aul started the engine. He was full from dinner and tired from all the wine. Little Joey and Monica were fighting in the back seat about the armrest. Monica wanted to use it as a pillow, Little Joey didn't want her hair on his side. Becky sat looking out the window. She didn't seem to hear the battle; somehow it never seemed to bother her that the kids fought. But it broke Paul's heart. Families are meant to be close. Brothers and sisters are meant to love each other. Why couldn't Monica and Little Joey just be friends?

Paul had an older sister named Mary who died of cancer when he was ten years old. He could still remember the smell of that hospital and the sound of his sister's labored breathing just before she slipped away. He'd never forget the emptiness of the house when they came home without her. The loneliness. Paul loved Mary, they had been fiercely close, and life without a sister seemed impossible. But he managed. He had to. His parents needed him to be strong and so he didn't cry at her funeral. He didn't cry at all. He was afraid that crying would tear something open inside him that he would never be able to fix. So he put the pain away, where it couldn't hurt him, and focused on his mom and dad.

There was a lot of activity around the Jones house for the first month or two after the funeral—they needed people to help fill Mary's void. But eventually the people went home and the Jones family was left with Mary's absence. His mother, once so young and pretty, dried into an old woman. She spent her time sleeping, often with Mary's pillow clutched in her arms. Paul's father wasn't around much. He claimed to be working, but Paul knew he was avoiding them. Both parents suffered and neither had the strength for the other's pain.

The divorce was quick. One minute Paul lived in his child-hood home, the next he was in a penthouse apartment with his father or an isolated beach house with his mother, surrounded by strange things and lost to himself. He was shuttled back and forth — a childhood spent trying to revive his parents. His identity hung on the success of the Jones family unit. Of course they never reunited. Some things just can't be fixed. Beth and Robert Jones both died when Paul was in his early twenties. Not only did he fail in his efforts to save their marriage, he never even made a dent in the crippling sorrow that finally stole both of their lives. Paul stumbled into adulthood with an overwhelming desire to please, a tremendously large inheritance and a terrible sense of loss. But now he had his own family.

"Please, guys." Paul turned in his seat and looked at his angry children. "We've had a lovely evening. Let's not fight, okay? I love you both so much."

"Ignore them." Becky reached over and turned on the radio. "Let's get home." Becky searched for a station she liked then cranked up the volume.

Paul turned, put the car in gear and drove his family home.

12

Angela Takes a Ride

Angela couldn't sit still. The Wentworths were better than she imagined: that house, those things, the manners, the maids—a lot of maids. She turned in her seat and said, "They are all so fantastic, Conrad."

Conrad drove as if he hadn't heard her.

"I love Norman. He's quiet but seems so nice." Angela touched his knee. Maybe she would give him a blowjob right now. "And your sister. Paul seems like a really good father to those kids. Such a nice family."

Conrad drove on.

"Thank you, sweetheart, for taking me." She moved her hand higher on his thigh. "I couldn't have enjoyed it more."

Conrad put his foot down on the gas pedal. They were speeding down Sunset. He was obviously mad, freezing her out again. What the hell had she done this time? She had barely uttered a word—as instructed—and she'd kept her attention focused on him exclusively. She'd done the hot and bothered show whenever he gave her the look. A perfect performance. No, Angela hadn't done anything, it was Conrad. He was such a moody guy but nothing a little sex wouldn't fix.

"Darling," Angela said. She ran her hand up and down his inner thigh. "Why don't we go to your house for a change?"

"No chance." Conrad accelerated around a corner.

"But it's Saturday." Angela leaned over and whispered in his ear. "We could hang out in bed. Have Alison come over? Maybe get out the video camera?"

"Nope." Conrad removed Angela's hand and down shifted as he came to the intersection. The engine roared.

"Okay," Angela said in her cheeriest voice. "We can stay at my house." She put her hand back on his leg, this time a little higher. "I'll run you a bath."

"Not gonna happen." The light changed and Conrad gunned the engine. He would have her home in minutes.

"Sweetie," Angela said as she started to unhook his belt. "What does 'not gonna happen' mean exactly?"

"I'm not coming in."

"I can make you feel so good." She unzipped his pants. "You know I can."

"Stop it." Conrad turned onto her street and hit the gas. They we going almost fifty. "This is getting really old, you know?"

Angela took her hand back. She could see her house up the block and she knew this was going to be bad. Wouldn't it be nice if she were in a normal relationship where the man and woman loved each other with a healthy balanced respect? Equal partners longing to explore the beauty of marriage and family with hope and joy and great expectations? Why couldn't she ever find a guy like that? Conrad pulled the car up to the curb. Angela braced herself and waited.

"I realized it tonight when I saw you with my family." Conrad turned his head and looked at her for the first time since they'd climbed in the car. "You're just not the type of girl who would really ly fit in. You know what I mean? Your background doesn't mesh with ours. I mean, you look the part, but when it comes down to it, when you actually open your mouth, you just don't pull it off. Not that that's bad. You're one of the hottest little numbers I had in a long time, and I'm sure there's plenty of guys out there who'd appreciate you, but for me it's not working on a cultural level, you know?" Conrad pulled the emergency brake and put the car in neutral. "You should find someone more on your level."

That class card was the one thing Angela was defenseless against. He must have sensed it the minute he met her. Was it that obvious? Angela spent her life working to fill in the gaps. She took a deep breath. She would not let him win.

"Excuse me, my lord," Angela said in her best British accent. "I've forgotten my place. How presumptuous of me to think that someone of your stature could possibly love me?" She wanted to scratch his eyes out but she keep a smile on her face and played the joke.

"There's no way I would ever marry someone like you. You must know that." Conrad rolled down the window. "So really there is no point in going any further, is there?"

"Actually there is." Angela felt like she'd just stepped out of a tenth story window. She was falling and she needed a plan before she hit the ground. She needed to regain control. Fast.

"I'm sure there's a lot of guys who could appreciate a gal like you." Conrad leaned across and pushed open the passenger door. "Bye bye, Angela Simms."

Good. Now he'd made her angry. Angela was once again in control. "It would be nice if I just quietly went away wouldn't it?" Angela smoothed her skirt. "There are two problems, Conrad. One, I love you. I'm sure they all say that to you, but in my case it happens to be true. And, number two . . ." Here she paused. She knew before she even said it that this was the wrong context but what the hell. "Number two is that I'm pregnant with your child."

"Bullshit."

"Our baby."

"Not mine."

"A little Wentworth."

"I got cut years ago." Conrad let out a bitter laugh, leaned across her and opened the passenger door. "Get out."

Angela had not been with anyone other than Conrad. His lie made her feel strong. "Conrad junior." She patted her stomach. "Or Connie."

"You really think this is going to work?"

"I haven't slept with anyone else."

"Get out of the car," Conrad said. "Now."

Angela got out. This is not how she'd planned things. In a perfect world he would have been excited and they could have shared a beautiful evening. But this world was not perfect and nothing had ever been easy in Angela's life. She was going to have to fight. She closed the door and leaned in the window. "This is your child and it's not going to go away."

Conrad shifted the car into gear, released the brake and hit the gas. Angela stood on the curb and watched him drive away.

13

Norman on His Big Brother

There is no question that my brother, Conrad Wentworth, is missing several strands of his DNA and it's my strong suspicion that Judith is, in some way, responsible. Maybe during those first few months of life, when she was fawning over his absolute perfection, marveling at the beauty of his unblemished body, fondling his superb genitalia and cleaning his sweet little asshole, maybe during that time she somehow cauterized an intrinsic part of his molecular composition. I don't know the details, that chapter has been lost or destroyed, but I can tell you with great certainty that by the time I was born Conrad had already been transformed from a human being into a cold-blooded reptile, a Gila monster if you will, or better yet a Komodo dragon, blood thirsty and cold. The transformation is apparently irreversible. Conrad spits and his bite is highly venomous. He will tear you limb from limb. Stay out of his way.

Conrad played one game with me and my sister when we were growing up. It was his game. He called it "Kitty in the Well" and it was the only time he paid us any attention. Of course playtime only happened when the parents were out of the house and one of the less responsible maids was left in charge. First he brought out the sleeping bag. I can remember my feelings of fear but also excitement at the mere sight of that brown nylon bag.

"Okay, my little kitties," Conrad would say in his nicest voice. "Time to hide."

Becky and I would tear off down the hall, searching frantically for a new place, one where Conrad would never think to look. Oh the thrill and the overwhelming dread. My sister and I would jam ourselves into cupboards or crawl up onto the top shelves of closets, under beds, behind curtains. And there we'd wait, barely breathing, hoping we wouldn't be found but knowing that eventually we would. That was the fun part of the game, the waiting, because once you were discovered the fun was over.

"Filthy kitty." Conrad would throw open the closet door and yell, "I'm allergic to cats."

Then he'd fling us over his shoulder, carry us down the hall, and stuff us into that old brown sleeping bag. He used a piece of rope to tie off the opening. The first child to get caught sometimes had a long and scary wait in that dark bag. I remember worrying about running out of oxygen. More than once I wet my pants. Eventually he'd find the other kitty, stuff us both in the nylon prison and then his fun began.

"Time to throw the kitties in the well." He'd drag us slowly down the hallway towards the back-stairs. The back-stairs were carpeted, the front stairs were stone. That was the only kindness Conrad showed us, he always used the back-stairs.

"What this world doesn't need are more filthy kitties."

Becky and I were smushed together, side-by-side. There was no room to move in that bag and the feelings of claustrophobia and panic were unbearable. "Help," we'd scream at the top of our lungs.

"Is that what kitties say?" Conrad would ask. "No. Does the kitty say moooo? No. Does the kitty say bow-wow? Noooo. What does the kitty say?"

And then we'd meow. Meow, meow, meow, meow, hoping to please him, hoping that he wouldn't throw us down the stairs, hoping that he'd untie the rope and let us breathe, or that if he did throw us down the stairs, he'd come down immediately afterward and let us out.

But the meowing never worked. Conrad always shoved us down those stairs, usually head first. We'd slide down fast like a load of lumber. Sometimes an elbow or a knee would snag on a step but that was bad because then Conrad would pull us back up and start the whole thing over. He liked to see us hit the bottom, hard. And then, once we were out of our minds with terror, he'd walk away and we would be left to scream our hearts out until one of the maids heard us and came to the rescue.

14

Conrad Wentworth, Fully Intact Male

This happened one other time because Conrad does not believe it's his responsiblity—that birth control shit. It's the woman's problem. This chick got knocked up early in the relationship, tried to jump on Conrad's gravy train. Didn't go over so well. Long story short—termination. Don't ever try and pull something on Conrad Wentworth 'cause your life is gonna be shit after you fuck with him. This guy don't take nothing from no one. And he don't give nothing away, neither. Nothing. He's decent. Just don't fuck with him. You don't want to make him angry.

The mistake Conrad made, the reason for this potential quagmire? He took her home. Why does he do that? It might be that mother thing but don't talk to Conrad about that Oedipus shit. He'll kill you. Don't even think about it in the same room with him 'cause the guy can read minds. He can look at you and see the thoughts playing across your eyeballs clear as a drive-in movie. Anyway, it's not like Conrad looks at his mother and gets hard. Nothing sick like that. It's deeper. Primal. Conrad wasn't breast fed because Judith didn't want to mess up her figure. Don't laugh, it was damaging. Baby bottles are very destructive. Ever wonder why kids throw them on the floor? You come into the world and the only thing you want is to be held against the warm body of your mother and to suckle at the all-encompassing breast. Is that too much to ask? Conrad didn't get that, not even once. He was bundled up and shipped off to a series of nurses who pumped him full of formula while his mother starved herself until the milk dried up and her body returned to its former skeletal self. Deny a guy those first ecstatic moments with the breast and he's going to spend the rest of his life looking for it. And he's not going to be happy either. Poor little Conrad, cried himself to sleep each night in that over-decorated nursery. He'd lie there on his little back, in the prison of that crib, staring at the goddamn teddy bear mobile going round and round, crying for his mama. Pretty tough stuff. Heartbreaking, if you think about it. So is it really that surprising that the women Conrad dates look like Judith? No. It's perfectly understandable. He's just trying to make things right.

Still, he shouldn't take the girlfriends home. Now he's got a chink in his armor. This Angela knows where they live. She's been to the epicenter.

15

Next Day: Judith Enjoys Her Morning

The house was built in 1929 (two years after the California earthquake laws went into effect) and called Villa Contenta. Judith had fallen in love with it even before she and August were married. It was an Edwardian mansion, large even by Bel Air standards with ten bedrooms and twelve baths (not including servants quarters), a pool house, a guest cottage (where Norman had taken up permanent residence) and eight acres of land. There were great oak and maple trees in the front yard and the house was covered in creeping vines. Judith thought it looked like the perfect English country house and it was the home of her dreams. She convinced August that this was the place to raise their family and so he gave it to her as a wedding gift.

Judith sat in the north courtyard and rejoiced in the fresh morning air. Not much had changed in the almost forty-five years since they'd moved here. The trees were taller, the garden more mature, but when she looked around the yard she felt as if she were still that newlywed, that young girl waking in the midst of a fairy tale. Judith went to sleep a pauper and awoke one morning to find herself a queen. And this, this Villa Contenta, was the kingdom over which she would rule, with a firm but just hand, for the rest of her life.

Judith sat at the round glass table by the Tuscan fountain and picked up the morning paper. Bad news, always bad, bad news. Judith was getting to the point where she simply couldn't stomach it anymore. The outside world was coming apart at the seams. It was so upsetting. The Muslims and the Jews, why couldn't those people just figure it out? Homicide, genocide, famine, drought, nuclear weapons and toxic waste. Honestly, it made one want to pull up the drawbridge and bolt the doors. Judith carefully folded the paper and put it back in its place. She would not let troublesome international affairs spoil this perfectly lovely morning. No, she had too many things to do today. Judith rang the small silver bell, time for breakfast. She leaned back in her chair, closed her eyes and waited. The birds were singing in the trees, the fountain played delicately in the background. Lovely, lovely. Suddenly the gardener fired up that god-awful blower. Where was he? Judith looked around. Not close, probably down by the tennis court, but still that noise was so intrusive. A terrible sound. What happened to rakes? She thought about going down and giving him a piece of her mind but this was the third gardener in the last year and she didn't want to chance another walk out. Gardeners were a tricky breed, especially good ones. You had to be careful how you talked to them or they'd storm off like the prima donnas they were. No, Judith didn't want to ruin her day with another confrontation. She'd have Rosa go down and ask him to please stop until she finished eating.

Here came Rosa with the tray. Judith had been eating the exact same breakfast for twenty years: Two pieces of whole wheat toast, dry of course, half a grapefruit, coffee with nonfat milk and one cube of sugar. That one cube was the extent of her sugar intake for the day. It was her single indulgence and she took it early in the day so that the guilt from that minor slip up would prevent her from making any more extreme mistakes at lunch and dinner.

Rosa set the tray on the table. She poured the coffee into the cup as Judith surveyed her morning meal. Everything was in its place and there was a lovely tulip from the garden in a small, cut glass vase. But wait, something was missing.

"Rosa, where are the tongs?"

Rosa pretended she was confused.

"The tongs." Judith mimicked the pinching of tongs with her thumb and index finger. "To pick things up." Here Judith used her fingers to reach over and take a sugar cube. "Like sugar. Silver sugar tongs, you know." She dropped the cube in her coffee. "I use them every morning. We used them last night for coffee after the dinner party. They are a part of the coffee service. Where are they, Rosa?"

Judith could tell from blank look on Rosa's face that she knew exactly what Judith was talking about. These people were infuriating. Judith took a deep breath. The leaf blower whined in the distance. Judith could feel her wonderful morning slip away. "Don't play stupid with me." Judith pointed her index finger at the middle of Rosa's chest. "Tell me. NOW."

"They were gone when I cleared last night." Rosa clasped her hands almost in prayer. "I looked under the couches. I looked in the chairs. Nothing. I ask everyone. *Pero nadie sabe donde están. No es mi culpa* . . ."

"Stop that Spanish right now," Judith said. "You know I can't understand you when you speak like that."

"I don't know what happened." Now Rosa looked as if she might cry. "I asked Graciela and Carmenita. Blanca was not there. No one knows. I did not take them, missus. None of us did. We would not steal from you."

"We'll just have to tear this house apart until we find it." Judith stood. "Go get the girls. I want you to search every inch of the house while I search your rooms."

Judith got up and headed for the servants' quarters. She left her breakfast sitting on the table, untouched.

16

Norman's Day

*N*orman fashioned a loincloth from an old white pillowcase. The cotton was a poor substitution for skin and looked more biblical than tribal—Jesus was definitely not part of this scenario. No, Norman needed skin. Animal hide. But where? Where in the middle of Bel Air was he going to find a perfect pelt? Maybe kill a squirrel? Bash it with a rock. Or a little dog? Norman rubbed his body with fragrant Kukui nut oil. It soothed him. The Goldblum's cat from next door had lovely orange fur. Perhaps he could lure the creature with a dish of tuna then drown it in the swimming pool. He could stretch the pelt across his crotch, run the tail through his legs and tie it at the back. A fur thong. A kitty G-string. Maybe hollow out one of the legs and use it as a sheath like the warriors of New Guinea. Leave part of the bone at the end of the leg to impress neighboring tribes. But a cat's front legs are too small. Would a back leg be wide enough? Norman pulled his semi-erect penis from his loincloth and looked at it. No, a cat wouldn't do. A dog's legs would be good, a big German Shepherd, but the fur wasn't as soft. Wait, if he wanted to feel the fur, he'd have to wear the skin inside out. Maybe he could line the dog with a cat so it would be fluffy and doubly warm. The idea made him smile, just one more piece of evidence that Norman should have gone into fashion. Norman Wentworth, genius. He poured more oil from the bottle and worked it into what was now a full-blown erection. The smell of the oil took him back into the deep jungle. Snakes and vines and darkness. He was a predator in this savage land, top of the food chain. His body glistened in the artificial light of his room. Drums were beating in Norman's head. Tribal drums. Loud and fierce. They were calling him, the constant pulse. BOOM, boom, boom, boom, BOOM, boom, boom, boom. And then he heard it:

"NORMAN," Judith yelled and pounded. "OPEN THIS DOOR."

17

What is the Meaning of This?

When Norman opened the door, Judith saw that his body was coated in some kind of oily lubricant and he was wearing an old sheet wrapped around his privates like a ridiculous diaper. She didn't even want to think about what he'd been doing.

"For God's sake," she said. "Cover yourself."

"Sorry." Norman darted inside. Judith forced herself not to look into the cottage. She just didn't want to know. She tried not to think about this part of Norman's life but sometimes it took her breath away. This boy, her baby boy, so beautiful and kind but so, so damaged. What went on in that head of his? What kind of strange world did he live in? What did he do out here in the guest-house all day long? Most of the time Judith was able to block it out. Most times she could pretend that Norman was simply a homosexual—unfortunate but not unusual. She tried to convince herself that he spent his days designing women's clothing or shoes like other queers, sketching away, exercising his undeniable creativity. She liked to think that he read a lot. Norman was intelligent. He was a movie buff and she thought he probably watched a lot of videos. But when she stumbled upon him in moments like this, when she interrupted one of his weird rituals and got a glimpse of the strange fantasy life he'd so carefully constructed, she wanted to fall to her knees and weep. Why couldn't Norman just be normal?

"I was practicing yoga." Norman returned to the door with a large bath towel wrapped around his body like a strapless evening gown. "A very ancient form, pre-khundalini. Not many people are familiar with it but I find the physical and spiritual..."

"Norman," Judith snapped. She could not bear to hear another word of his charade. It was just too painful and grotesque. She closed her eyes for a moment and cleared her head. Focus, she needed to focus. There was a job to do. She opened her eyes and started again. "My sugar tongs are missing. They're valuable. Do you have them?"

"No." Norman crossed his arms over his towel-clad chest.

"Do you know where they might be?" Judith hated it when he was difficult. She wasn't accusing *him*.

"Nope." He was playing with his fingernails now. "Ask the maids."

"Of course I've asked the maids." Judith reached out and stopped him from pulling on a hangnail. "We've torn the house apart."

"Well." Suddenly Norman had made both wrists go limp. "If it was me, I'd call the Joneses. I'd ask for a thorough search of Joey's and Monica's rooms. I'd pull up floorboards, break through walls. I might even insist on a backhoe for the yard. If it was me, that's where I'd start my search for the missing tongs. The Jones' house."

"Norman Wentworth." How dare he implicate her grand-children? Pathetic fool. He was just jealous because he didn't have children of his own. Judith clenched her teeth and forced herself not to raise her voice. "If I ever hear you say another disparaging word about my grandchildren, or any other family member, there will be hell to pay. Do you hear me? This lifestyle of yours could be gone in an instant." Here Judith snapped her fingers to demonstrate just how quickly she could ruin his life. "We are family and we stick together." Judith glared at him, held his eyes and would not let him look away.

Finally he said, "I'm sorry."

"You better be sorry. Now get dressed and look around. Maybe you took them home with you last night, by mistake." Judith headed back to the house. She'd tried to reach Gus at the country club but he wasn't there. She would have to try again.

18

*Norman Escapes from
Judith and Goes to
the Department Store*

As Judith ages, her sight narrows. And while her distance perception is shot, she's developed 20/20 tunnel vision. She focuses only on the things that please her. Hers is a near perfect world and she defends it mercilessly. No ugly reality mars her day-to-day existence. When we family members drift into her view, she sees what she needs to see. She wouldn't, couldn't allow herself to know who we really are. A gay son would be a dark spot on her horizon. Her morally bankrupt eldest son would signal high seas and hurricane force winds, an absolute catastrophe. And the dysfunction of Becky, of the entire Wentworth-Jones family—well the shock of it could permanently blind my poor mother. In her world, if you don't acknowledge a problem, then it doesn't exist—that's Judith's recipe for tranquility. Wouldn't it be wonderful if someone could invent spectacles that would force her to see the big picture? Glasses that wouldn't let her look away. How would it be for Judith to walk around seeing others for who they really are and not just in relationship to herself? What would she do when reality forced itself past her barriers? Judith Wentworth, as just another human being on this huge earth, no more or less important than anyone else. How would she handle that? She would collapse. It would kill her to live in the world that the rest of us inhabit. Her lungs would shut down, her heart would stop beating, she'd have a fatal stroke. Absolute implosion followed by a wee bit of smoke. No, Judith couldn't take it.

Enough. Enough, enough, enough. This is my day, my time and I will not let her ruin it. Shoes. Sportswear. Accessories. Comfort lies somewhere close by.

This department store is a kind of sanctuary for me, a true spiritual retreat. Attractive people buying expensive things, everyone is happy, the outside world far away. Floor after floor of things I need and if I get tired I can take the elevator to the top and have a delicious lunch surrounded by all sorts of celebrities. Coming here gives me such satisfaction and sense of purpose. And yet, today, Judith and her tongs keep sneaking in. I bet she's conducting a full inspection of my room right now. Cavity searches for the staff. Lie detectors. Truth serum. Never mind.

Here we are at the fragrance counter and it's offering us the assurance of a fresh start. Improved opportunity. I enjoy the rawness of the male scent. I can detect the acrid sharpness of a sweaty man from a mile away. It calls to me; we are animals, after all. But I can also appreciate male enhancers: cologne, eau du toilette. Nothing like a good shower and a new smell for attracting attention. And I love the names: Pulse, Crave, Ultraviolet Man, Mambo, Red Tide, Fahrenheit One, Chrome, North Dakota. Every pot has its lid. But there's danger in these parts. Each "sales associate" is working on a commission. They desperately need you to buy their product and will lift their arms and madly spray you with their scent if you're not quick enough with a refusal. Wave them off because the combination of all these smells will result a skunk-like odor that may necessitate a long soak in tomato juice. Trust me, you have to be selective. Let's move on.

There's nothing more exciting than the promise of a new skin care line. Who among us hasn't stood in front of the mirror and

eagerly awaited the firming and tightening of the jowls and troubling under-eye area that is promised by the latest antioxidant, col-
lagen enhancing salves and ointments. We've all troweled on the
night cream and waited for those fine lines to fade away. Is this foul
smelling cream made from crushed up foreskins the miracle I've
been waiting for? Will the goat collostrum from China ease my
marionette lines? How do I regain that dewy freshness? Where is
that next scientific breakthrough? It's all so exciting.

And so I head to the cosmetic counter and allow the sales
woman to work her magic. She'll start by telling me what amazing
skin I have. That's to make me feel comfortable. Then she'll lean
in and sadly discover that I do have a little sun damage and the
beginnings of dullness. We will both struggle with this tough news
for a moment, but then she will brighten as she informs me that,
just last week, she received a new product that will solve all my
problems and take ten years off my face. Ten years. Do I really
want to look that young? Oh, what the hell, of course I do. And
out come the samples. She cleanses me, she tones me, she moistur-
izes and sun screens me. She even applies lip balm. But her touch
is not gentle and I do not feel soothed and so I tell her I will think
about it. I leave her counter disappointed, without spending a
dime, and make my way to the shoe department.

19

Conrad Takes the Call

"No idea, Mother."

"They're very valuable. You remember we got them in Vienna."

"Yeah, you told me."

"What about your friend?"

"Angela."

"Maybe she got them by mistake."

"I don't think so."

"They're somewhere, Conrad. Things don't just disappear. They are sitting in a very specific location at this very moment and we need to find out where that is. I want them back."

"I know Mother."

"Ask her."

"Who?"

"Your friend."

"Angela."

"She should check her purse and pockets."

"She didn't take them."

"She might have, accidentally. Call her."

"We broke up last night."

"No, really? She was such a pretty girl. And nice."

"No."

"She wasn't nice?"

"Gold-digger."

"Maybe she stole the tongs."

"I don't think so mother. Did you check Norman?"

"He hasn't seen them."

"But did you actually check? He may have turned your tongs into a tiara or something."

"I hate it when you do that. Norman did not take the tongs. Why can't you be a little nicer to your brother? They've done studies, you know. Homosexuals are born that way. It isn't his fault . . ."

"You're right Mother. I'm sorry."

"Please call that woman and ask her to check for the tongs. I have a feeling she has them. Please."

"All right, Mother."

"Promise."

"I swear."

20

Becky

*B*ecky had just finished covering her face with the Miracle Noir Moisturizing Mask composed of secret ingredients culled from the Dead Sea. It was greasy, made with some sort of inky mud and when she looked in the mirror she saw herself black-faced and unrecognizable. She wondered for a moment: what would it be like to be an African American? But that wasn't a thought that held Becky's interest. She dropped her robe and turned her attention to a thorough inspection of her body. She stood facing the mirror with her ankles together and studied her legs. The knees just barely touched each other and there was a good three inches between her thighs. Very important to maintain that space between the thighs. It was how she measured her thinness. If that margin dropped below two inches she would stop eating and begin her special fast where she consumed nothing but Dieter's Tea until she regained her desired three inches. Becky had been good lately, she'd barely touched her dinner this evening, and her whole body was bony and drawn. She kept herself well waxed so there wasn't a sign of hair. She hated hair. It's true that the area between her legs wasn't quite what it once was, before the children, but the skin still retained enough firmness that she found herself slightly aroused by the sight of her neat cleft. Becky felt sexy. She turned from the mirror and was about to step into her luxurious warm bath and enjoy the Epicurean

Aromatherapy Wild Lavender Bath Salts when the phone rang.

The problem at her house was that Becky was the only one who ever answered the phone. Paul feigned deafness whenever it rang, Monica was shut in her room with the music blasting, and anyway her friends always called her on the cell phone so why would she bother? And Little Joey apparently didn't have any friends. So it fell to Becky or Lucy, the housekeeper, to answer the damn thing every time it rang. Well, Lucy would just have to deal with it, Becky was going to enjoy her bath.

"Missus Becky," Lucy called from the bottom of the stairs.

Becky filled her lungs with air then shouted, "Take a message." But Lucy could barely speak English. "No, never mind. Give the phone to Paul."

Becky slid into the yummy water and admired once again how thin her legs and stomach looked. Why, she looked like a young girl. Her body was much sexier than Monica's. She could probably pass for a teenager, a young girl who all the boys admired, who all the boys wanted, who all the boys dreamed about at night. None of the other girls had a body like hers. None of the other girls could stay so thin, so free of ugly fat and loose flapping thighs. No, Becky was in a class all her own and the boys loved her and the jealous girls hated her. Becky ran her hand along her inner thighs and felt that delicious melting heat between her smooth legs. She closed her eyes and saw that Cushner boy who lived down the street. He was a couple of years older than Monica and drove her to school each morning. That Cushner boy had the body of an Adonis. Young muscles. Tanned. What would he look like here in the bathtub? How would his skin feel as she soaped his body?

Paul burst into the bathroom holding the portable phone.

"Why can't you knock, fathead?" Becky crossed her legs and sat up in the tub. "Privacy? Personal space? It's not that difficult, Paul."

Paul held out the phone in a pathetic offer of peace. "Your mother."

Becky wiped her wet hand on Paul's pant leg and took the phone. "Mom?"

"I can't find my tongs." Judith was very upset.

"Tongs?"

"The antique silver tongs from Vienna. For sugar cubes."
Judith talked very fast. "We used them last night."

Monica put the washcloth over her crotch so Paul would stop
staring. "Did you ask Rosa?"

"We've torn the house apart."

"Maybe one of the other maids. They're valuable."

"The help knows better."

"What about that woman of Conrad's?"

"Becky, stop that."

"What? She's a preschool teacher. I mean, come on."

"Conrad would never bring a thief into the house." Judith
raised her voice another octave. "You've got to work on that
jealousy. You've always been jealous of your brother. It's very unat-
tractive. Get a handle on it."

Becky held her breath. It's what she did when her mother
treated her this way. She felt five years old again. How could her
mother make her feel so bad? Why did she do it? Becky bit her lip
and fought the pressure in her lungs. Finally she blew out the air
and said, "I don't know, Mother. I'm sorry about your tongs."

"Ask the children. Check everyone's pockets."

"What are you saying?" Becky brought her knees to her chest.
"Are you accusing us?"

"Don't be ridiculous. They could have accidentally fallen into
a pocket of a purse. Just look around. It's important to me."

Becky hung up and handed the phone back to Paul.

"What?" Paul was helplessly nosy. He had a very bad habit of
eavesdropping on phone conversations. It drove Becky mad.

"Nothing. She can't find her fucking tongs." Becky closed her
eyes and slid down into her bath. "Close the door on your way out."

Becky tried to go back to the Cushner boy but he was lost to
her. The bath water was getting cold and the dinner party kept
replaying itself over and over. Judith and Conrad, as usual.
Sometimes she hated her mother. Becky pulled the plug and let the
water drain out of the tub.

21

Elephants Don't Forget and Neither Does Norman

Memories, like the corners of my mind . . ." I have a nice voice, don't I? "Misty watercolor memories . . ." When we were children, my mother loved to hear me sing. She insisted that Becky and I perform whenever there were guests in our home. Who knows where Conrad was? Mostly I remember Christmas songs, is that possible? Did she really have us singing "Silent Night" in September? "Jingle Bells" at Easter? Quite possibly. I was shy until the song got underway and then, once the music took hold, I felt encumbered by my virtually tone-deaf sister. God, I hated Becky's voice. Have you ever heard the shrieks of quarreling seagulls dive-bombing the carcass of a rotting sea lion? The cries of a dog whose pelvis has been destroyed by a speeding car? My sister and I would stand by the fireplace, hands clasped in front. Usually we were dressed in matching his/hers outfits, often with a cheery spring-time or nautical theme. I may be gay but I didn't appreciate being dressed like a fairy, even at that tender age. I became a big fan of purple grape juice once I realized its tremendous staining capacities. Many a Peter Pan collar was destroyed by a big glass of Welch's. Anyway, we would stand there in front of our doubtlessly embarrassed audience and sing two or three songs until Judith tired of the show and sent us off to bed. I can remember hoping that Becky would go upstairs alone so I could belt out a couple of solos, but I don't believe that ever happened.

Becky is older than me. Of course you knew that, it's obvious. She's two years older and when you're a little boy, that's significant. Sometimes when we were children she treated me as her pet, her babydoll, her precious, precious love. She dressed me in her old Tinkerbelle outfits, made-up my face, included me at her tea parties with Barbie, the stuffed animals and the trolls. She painted my fingernails and tried to style my hair. Often I wore her fancy Easter hats. I loved those hats, they were right out of *Go Dog Go*: "Hello. Hello. Do you like my hat? No I do not like your hat. Goodbye. Goodbye." Becky and I would sit there, in those tiny white wooden chairs, sipping imaginary tea and eating invisible cookies, talking with the plastic and furry figurines about their complicated lives and the challenges they faced. She had an enormous dollhouse in the corner of her room and we were constantly putting sick children to bed and calling the doctor. There was always a chance that someone might die. Or else we would get Barbie ready for her date with Ken. Would Barbie let Ken kiss her? Not on a first date, no way on a first date. Barbie had a big wardrobe. My job was to fold and put away her dresses, organize the Barbie carrying case and keep track of the Barbie high heels. I loved those tiny pumps! They were nice afternoons, just Becky and me, ideally suited to my young temperament. Nice until Judith snuck up and pounced upon us. Mother would throw open the door, gasp in horror, and reprimand me for not being manly enough. I lacked that incessant male need to yell, pound my chest and constantly destroy things. Why wasn't I outside climbing trees and pulling wings off butterflies, like other boys? Why didn't I like football or hockey? Maybe because I was only six. Mother would send me out to play in the yard and Becky would be taken aside for yet another heart-to-heart talk. Usually, after one of Judith's raids, Becky treated me like a freak and I was left to play on my own. Sometimes my exile would last for a couple of weeks.

Becky struggled with her weight during her early childhood. She wasn't fat, she was a normal and healthy little girl, but Judith and August thought her pudgy. August cleverly nicknamed her "Fats" and Judith spent the day policing Becky's portion size and food selections. By the time Becky hit puberty, she was a goner— a lifetime of eating disorders, guaranteed. Thankfully that was one area I escaped criticism. I've always had a brilliant metabolism.

My sister got older, started to develop, and without much prompting from Judith stopped inviting me into her room. She would slam her door in my face, lock it, and tell me to go away, calling me a poof or a fruit or a faggot. For a long time I told myself that this was just another game we were playing, a game that I hadn't yet mastered.

When Becky started junior high, she talked the parents into putting a phone extension in her room. I found that if I laid flat on the carpet and wedged my ear to the crack at the bottom of the door, I could hear pretty much everything she said. It was thrilling, listening to her read the note that Johnny or Tommy or Billy had passed to her in social studies class. "Will you go to second base with me? Yes. No. Maybe. Check one." Becky would squeal and giggle. I didn't always know what she was talking about but I always found it fascinating. It went on for a long time, her chatting and me listening until she caught me there late one afternoon. She threw her door open and before I had a chance to stand up she kicked me in the head so hard that my ear bled. She screamed about me being a freak until mother came running. I remember there was a trip to the emergency room. I don't think she caused any permanent damage to my brain, but you never know.

22

The Night: Becky Can't Sleep Even With Two Sleeping Pills

I don't know who took the tongs. Frankly I don't care, but I'll tell you one thing: I don't trust Conrad. I actually think he's a little evil. He doesn't care about anyone but himself. He's capable of doing anything. He might have taken those tongs just to stir things up, make someone look bad. And why hasn't he ever married? I don't think you should trust men over forty who haven't married. I mean, there's a reason. Either they're secretly gay, or they're pathologically self-involved. But unfortunately, I'm the only one in the family that sees Conrad clearly. I mean, I don't know, maybe Norman sees it but Norman doesn't really count. Conrad has made a career out of sucking up to the parents. They're so proud of him, it makes me want to puke. He acts so sweet with mother. God, if only she could see the way he tenses when she takes his arm or pets his hair. That stony look he gets when he kisses her cheek. He is absolutely not interested in the latest acquisitions at the museum or the dinner-dance at the country club but to see him sitting there, listening to her, you'd think she was describing some live sex act with teenaged girls and a burly Great Dane. It makes me crazy that she can't see it. Judith has bought into his show 100 percent and so has August. Their son, the famous attorney. "Look, Conrad's in the paper again." August spends a good part of his day searching for more evidence of his eldest son's success. He brags about how Conrad is one of the highest paid attorneys in this city. But trust me, Conrad doesn't care about law. He certainly isn't interested in justice. I swear he went to law school just so, when the time came, he could screw Norman and me. And he will if he can.

The thing is, August isn't going to be around forever. I mean, my God, with his diet and the drinking? Look at him, he's a poster boy for heart disease, gout, diabetes, Lou Gehrig's disease, Alzheimer's, M.S., Parkinson's and God knows what else. Don't even get me started on the cancers. I keep looking for tremors or twitching, 'cause those are signs. So far nothing. But you gotta keep a look out. The real nightmare, the worst possible scenario would be if he has a stroke. Can you imagine? August in a wheel chair? Drooling? Diapers? Let me just say right here and now, I'm not changing any diapers. Never again. I will not be the one cleaning his foul old bottom, and I don't want Judith doing it either. You know Conrad's not going to do it. No. We'll hire someone and pray that that stage of August's life doesn't go on too long.

Anyway, that's why I keep getting on mother to do some planning. What's going to happen when August goes? What's the money situation? She should be informed. Shouldn't all women know exactly what to expect when their husbands kick? I want to know how the money's going to be split. Do we all get the same amount? I'm the only one that got married. I'm the only one with kids. Will that be taken into consideration? Seems like there should be some kind of reward. I want to know what the plan is for the grandchildren. August promised he'd pay for college. But is it in writing? We can't leave this to Conrad. Conrad would probably send Monica and Little Joey off to the local junior college or some technical school just to save a buck. No way. I want what's coming to me. My family needs to be taken care of and I want it in writing. I deserve it.

23

Next Morning: Paul Gets the Kids Up

The alarm went off at 6:30. Paul waited for Becky to swat the snooze button. BEEP, BEEP, BEEP, BEEP. He shook her shoulder. BEEP, BEEP, BEEP, BEEP. She insisted the clock be on her side of the bed. BEEP, BEEP, BEEP, BEEP. She hated it when he crawled over her. BEEP, BEEP, BEEP, BEEP.

"Becky," he rolled her onto her back. "Wake up, sweetie. The alarm."

Becky was sound asleep. Her mouth was slightly open and she made little snoring sounds on each intake of breath. There was drool on the pillow. This was not like her. She was the one that woke at the slightest disturbance and needed complete quiet to sleep. She was the one who forced Paul to get surgery for his snoring. She was the one who insisted he stop drinking fluids at seven o'clock in the evening so he wouldn't have to get up in the night. He wasn't allowed to read if he happened to have insomnia. In fact, she discouraged him from even moving in the bed until she had fallen fast asleep. No, Becky was not hard to rouse unless, of course, she'd gotten into the sleeping pills again.

Paul reached over her and turned off the clock. "Sweetheart, wake up."

Becky mumbled something, clutched her pillow, turned away from Paul and curled into a tight ball.

He unfolded her and gave her gentle slaps on the face. "Becky." Slap, slap. "Becky, what did you do?" Slap, slap, slap. "Did you take the pills again?" Here he grabbed both cheeks and shook her head.

Becky opened her eyes.

"Are you all right, sweetie?"

"Just tired." She started to roll up again.

"Did you take those pills again?"

"A couple." She pulled the pillow over her head. "I need to sleep. Mother and her fucking tongs."

Paul sighed. It was no use arguing with her when she was like this. She'd probably sleep till noon, then wake up and act as if nothing had happened. This pill thing was becoming a real problem. He didn't exactly know what to do. It was something he'd have to think about.

Paul put on his robe and slippers. He'd never been much of a pajama/bathrobe type of guy until he met Becky. He'd actually preferred sleeping in the nude, but Becky thought that indecent. On one of their first dates she marched him straight to Brooks Brothers and picked out appropriate PJs and a robe and Paul had been wearing them ever since. Still, the truth was, he preferred to sleep in the nude. He missed it.

Paul walked down the hall to Monica's room. Becky complained that Monica's door was always locked but it was unlocked this morning. He knocked twice and went in. Monica slept soundly in her pink canopy bed. They'd surprised her with it when she was in the fourth grade. A princess' bed for his darling angel. Monica had been thrilled and carried pictures of it to school. She used the bed as part of her school project, something about girls sleeping better when surrounded by pink. Paul looked at his little girl. She was so beautiful. He could see that she was becoming a young woman but watching her sleep, she still looked like that sweet little fourth grader who loved to sit in his lap.

"Mo-mo." Paul walked over to the bed. "How's my little angel?"

"Please don't call me that, Daddy." She pulled the sheet up over her naked shoulders.

Daddy, just like when she was a little girl. Paul loved *Daddy*. *Daddy* came from the days of Play Doh spaghetti and mud pies in the backyard and scary ghost stories with the endless search for a secret passage way or a hidden key. It was *Daddy* and Mo-mo who baked chocolate chip cookies together and ate the whole batch. (Becky had to be out of the house for that.)   It was a time when she'd hold his hand in public and really want to know what he thought. He was her *Daddy*, the most important man in her life, and she was his little angel. Why couldn't she be sweet like that anymore?

"Time to get up, sugar plum." He sat on the end of the bed and gave her foot a little squeeze. "Up and at 'em."

Monica sat up. "I can't get up until you leave." She yanked the sheet up around her neck. "I'm not exactly wearing anything. Do you mind?"

"No, no." Paul jumped up. He was suddenly embarrassed. "I'm sorry." He quickly left the room and closed the door behind him.

Little Joey's room was at the end of the hall. It was a long hall, lined with Becky's collection of cat prints and watercolors. Becky was crazy about cats. And highly allergic to them. Theirs was an animal-free home. Becky had never been able to tolerate any type of hairy pet, but she compensated by obsessively collecting feline images. She shopped for cat paintings wherever they went. One Christmas Paul had surprised her with a real Canadian hairless, a Sphynx, but Becky said the thing reminded her of an opossum with its almost reptilian pelt. She'd insisted they take the creature back to the pet store after only three days. She didn't want a real pet. Becky wasn't an affectionate person. She wasn't the type to curl up with her beloved "Fluffy" or "Cuddles" or "Muffin" or "Puss." She didn't dote on anything and she never spoke baby talk even to her own tiny babies. No, Becky was better served by artistic renderings, little two-dimensional furry kittens and bowls of milk. It was the image that pleased Becky, the illusion of the cat. The idea of a loving pet, represented in charming scenes around a blazing fire with balls of tangled yarn and laughing children or snowy evenings and window seats, a good book and a beautiful Persian cat curled in one's lap. This was the world that Becky brought home and hung on every square inch of blank wall.

Paul preferred dogs. As he walked down the hallway, he wondered again about the possibility of getting some sort of outdoor dog. It could live in the backyard. Paul would take care of it, walk it every morning and evening, feed and bathe it. Becky would hardly know it was there. He'd raised this possibility several times over the years and Becky was always adamantly opposed but now that Little Joey was getting older, he could help with the dog. It would be a good father/son bonding experience. A dog would bring them together.

Little Joey's door was locked, not unusual. Little Joey kept his door locked most of the time. Becky complained about Monica's door but she never mentioned Joey's. Why not?

"Joey." Paul knocked. "Hey, guy. Time to get up."

Paul worried about his relationship with Joey. The problem was, he didn't really have one. They spent time together at the breakfast table in the morning eating Lucy's eggs or French toast. Sometimes they'd agree that Lucy was the best cook in the world. Sometimes they'd finish each other's leftovers. But that wasn't a relationship, not really. Paul drove Joey to his middle school everyday. Seemed like that would have been a good time for heart-to-heart talks, just the two guys in the car alone—Monica was already off to high school—but Joey usually turned his body away, gripped the door handle as if he were just waiting to escape, and stared out the window. Paul had a hard time thinking of what to say to his son, and so most mornings they rode along in silence.

He'd tried to interest Joey in some sort of hobby, something they could do together—sports, model building, rock collecting—but nothing ever took. Paul and his father, God rest his soul, collected pennies. Paul still had the collection and he had offered it to his son but Joey wasn't interested so Paul let it go. (Where was that collection? Paul would have to look for it.) At night the family ate dinner together but those times usually consisted of Becky and Monica fighting over Monica's latest crime. Joey didn't say much at family dinners and neither did Paul. They were the spectators to the increasingly bloody battles. The boys kept their heads down, dutifully eating their food and dodging bullets. Once in a while Paul and Joey would make eye contact over a particularly stupid accusation, occasionally they would smile at each other, but mostly it was Joey eating his food, lost in his own world. He was a loner, quiet and withdrawn. Nothing wrong with that. It's just that Paul wished he knew his son better and he hoped that everything was all right. He would talk to Becky about a dog. He would insist. Paul knocked gently at the door.

Little Joey was awake. He listened to his father knock at the door. Paul was a tapper, tentative, as if he didn't want to disturb. Becky on the other hand was a banger. She took a locked door personally and attacked it with all of her strength. Little Joey lay curled in his bed, clammy sheets wrapped around his perspiration-damp pajamas. He nestled into the pillows and wondered how long his father would tap. The room was warm as an incubator and the curtains were all drawn. It was cozy and safe here and Little Joey wished his father would just go away.

"Joey." Paul rattled the door handle. Sometimes Paul dropped the *Little*, usually when he wanted something. "Joey. Unlock the door."

Little Joey wondered who would last longer, the pleading father or the sleeping son.

"Please son." Paul knocked again. "School."

Joey didn't want to go to school. School was the dullest place on earth. Maybe he'd take a sick day. Maybe he'd just ignore Paul and Paul would go away. Of course there was always the danger that Becky would get involved and then all hell would break loose. "Coming, Dad."

———

The room was stuffy and humid. The smell of sweat and dirty socks made Paul realize that Little Joey was becoming a man. Gosh, the time went fast.

"Beautiful day, son." Paul pulled up the shades and opened the windows as Little Joey climbed back into bed and pulled the pillow over his head.

"Five more minutes," Little Joey said. He was not a morning person.

Paul walked over and turned off the portable heater that Little Joey kept next to the bed. There was a half filled bottle of creme soda and an empty bag of barbecue potato chips. Becky would have a fit if she knew Little Joey was sneaking junk food into his room. But what was the big deal? All kids ate like this. Paul bent over to pick up the incriminating evidence. As he straightened up, he noticed a small tear in the mattress where the sheets had pulled off. He bent to take a closer look. It wasn't a tear, the mattress had been cut.

"What are you doing, Dad?" Little Joey swung his feet over the side of the bed and covered the hole with his legs.

"There's some sort of cut or tear . . ."

"Yeah, it's been like that for a while." Little Joey pulled the mattress cover down. "I was playing swords. Don't tell Mom."

"Swords?" Sounded like a pretty active game for Little Joey.

"When I was younger." Little Joey was up now and making his bed—something he never did as far as Paul knew. "I gotta get ready, Dad. I'll see you downstairs for breakfast."

A troubled Paul left the room. It wasn't like Little Joey to play with knives.

Paul dropped Little Joey off at school and drove back home. Usually those drives were conducted in silence with Paul asking the occasional question and Joey giving the one or two word answer, staring out the window. This morning Joey wouldn't shut up. He wanted to know about Paul's work at the investment firm, asked about the difference between state and federal income tax, wondered exactly how 401Ks worked. It just didn't make sense. So Paul parked the car in the garage and headed straight for Joey's room.

The bed was made with hospital-like precision. Paul didn't know that Little Joey was capable of such fastidiousness. He kneeled by the side of the mattress and tugged the bedding loose. This was no accident. The hole was a good four inched long and cut deep. Paul worked his fingers into the dense stuffing and found what seemed to be a hollowed cavity. A hiding place. What on earth did Little Joey have to hide? This was a kid who never left the house unless forced. What kind of trouble could be possibly be in? Was it drugs? Was Little Joey a drug addict? Paul felt around. Whatever he'd been hiding, it was gone now. Paul remade the bed as best he could and walked down the hall to his bedroom to see if Becky was awake. He didn't quite know what to do.

24

Norman's Jamboree

*B*oth my brother and sister participated in the Scouting program. Imagine cute Becky in her Brownie uniform and Conrad as an Eagle Scout. The uniforms were fantastic—so HJ (Hitler-Youth). And yes, the scouts do salute. What a lovely feeling it must have been to truly belong. Did you know that when you start the program as a Cub Scout you are a member of a Pack? A Pack can be quite large and so it is divided into smaller groups of six or eight boys, called Dens, and these smaller groups meet once a week with an adult who mentors them in the ways of scouting. The Pack usually meets once a month unless there's something special coming up, like a group campout or sing-a-long.

Cub Scouts go places and do things: crafts, games, sports, songs and puzzles, and of course badge work. Badge work is one of the principal elements in the overall scouting experience for both girls and boys. Cub Scouts work hard to obtain their Tiger Cub, Bobcat, Wolf, Bear, and Webelos badges. The ultimate honor, of course, is the Arrow of Light merit badge. With each badge, the uniform becomes more impressive. A young Cub with a chestful of badges is a proud boy indeed. Group goals include the Emergency Preparedness Award, Outdoor Activity Award and the all-important World Conservation Award. Busy Cub Scouts have global visions.

The neckerchief is essential and practical. It serves as an attractive part of the overall uniform but, when unrolled, it is also the perfect size for use as a triangular bandage during any first-aid emergency. You never know when someone is going to fall in the woods and impale themselves on a sharp stick. And, in cases of wilderness accidents, a well-trained scout in a neckerchief is exactly the person you want on hand. There are a number of neckerchief slides to help keep everything tidy. My favorite is the classic brass rounded-knot with the scouting eagle emblem, although the 3-hole leather neck-slide is also quite elegant.

Me? No, I was never a Scout. I wanted to be. As a very young boy, I dreamed of finally growing big enough to fit into my Cub Scout uniform and joining the troop. But although it was a good program for my brother and sister, Judith and August didn't think that I would fit in with the Boy Scouts of America. And so I was left to my own devices on Tuesday afternoons. I remember playing long games of tetherball out there on that asphalt playground, all by myself, waiting for one of the housekeepers to pick me up, while Troop 243 met next door in the community room. No matter, I'm fully versed in the program and I'm sure I can answer any questions you might have.

25

Angela Sims— Owner and CEO of Happy Helpers Preschool

Angela Simms stood behind the shiny red door and looked at her watch. 7:55. She could hear them out there, parents with the children. They'd been lined up since 7:30, eager to unload their kids. The same group showed up half an hour early every morning and stood there in the front yard with the stupid hope that maybe today would be different. Maybe today Angela—sweet Miss Angela —would be kind and let them get rid of their precious angels thirty minutes early. No dice.

Angela was in a very bad mood. She hadn't heard from Conrad in days. Motherfucker. She'd thrown up again this morning. Her fingers were swollen. She was tired and there was just the faintest hint of that dreaded estrogen mask on her upper lip and chin. Also, she was hung-over. Fucking pregnancy.

8:02. Another minute or so, one of the parents would tap on the door. They had to get to work, didn't Angela understand? There were appointments and meetings and urgent documents to be signed. These were parents with lives that mattered and they couldn't waste any of their oh-so-valuable time waiting outside a preschool. When she opened the door, they'd place one hand over the cell phone, give little Clay or Yoko or Zoë a gentle shove into the school, and say, "Gotta run. Big day." And then, on retreat, "Bye honey, I love you. Thanks Angela." You could tell they were pissed but no one ever confronted Angela directly. They didn't want to anger her because, who knows, then maybe little Connor or Madison or Beau wouldn't get to make potato prints or use the blunt tip scissors or sit on the teacher's lap.

Of course it was a completely different story on the other end. None of these people worried about her schedule when the day was done. Most of them sent nannies to do the pickup and the nannies didn't seem to be able to tell time. 2:00 Los Angeles time translated into 2:30 or even 3:00 Latin American time. No matter. She charged late fees, one dollar per minute, and the school made quite a nice profit on penalties alone.

8:03. What the hell. Angela put on her teacher face—a face that was perpetually excited, enchanted and invariably kind. Her face said, "I love these children as much as you do. Maybe more. And I'm a professional so I understand them in a way that you never will." Her face said, "Trust me. I know what's best." Her face said, "I promise never to raise my voice. Can you parents make that same claim?" Hers was a face of authority and wisdom. Angela took a deep breath. She would much rather be on a yacht cruising the Mediterranean or at a spa getting mud baths or even at home in bed. Anywhere but here. Angela secured her smile and opened the red door to let the children in.

26

What Now, Gus?

Gus sat in his car outside Honey's apartment. It was early afternoon, time to go home. Time to walk into his house, his castle, kick off his shoes and order someone to bring him a drink or a sandwich or the newspaper and his glasses. Time to look interested while Judith recited the inane details of her endless day. Time to wander from room to room trying to remember what exactly it was he was looking for. And then it would be time to change for dinner. Time to drive Judith to the country club where they would spend the evening with people just like themselves. His childhood friend David had died recently and they were taking his widow Maggie for dinner. Another one of their group gone. It was almost unbearable if he thought about it, so he didn't. Tonight August would drink the cocktails, stand with the other men, tell jokes and pretend that time wasn't passing, everything was as it should be. Dinners like these were the mainstay of Gus' life. They were predictable and safe and usually he looked forward to them. But this afternoon Gus just sat in his car. He didn't want to go home. He certainly didn't want to go back inside to Honey. God, no. He'd given Honey Belmont a thorough thrashing and frankly he was exhausted.

Gus took his hands off the steering wheel and rested them in his lap. They were covered with brown age spots and the skin was papery thin. There was a dark purple bruise on his right knuckle and a cut on his left thumb that didn't want to heal. How had he gotten these injuries? Gus had no idea. His body was becoming more and more fragile and if he stopped to think about it, it scared him. August Wentworth sat in the front seat of his car and couldn't think of where to go. He sat there with his hands in his lap and picked at the age spots and the bruise.

27

More Introductions:
The Belmonts

$\mathcal{H}$ONEY BELMONT was not her real name. Originally she was Mary Beth Lafont from Salt Lake City, the daughter of Benjamin and Ruth Lafont, good Mormons who harbored certain curiosities about the purer practices of the Fundamentalist Latter Day Saints. When Benjamin died of untreated diabetes, Ruth quickly remarried and became the fourth wife of a well-respected polygamist named Eliot Lawrence, and little six-year-old Mary Beth Lafont became Mary Beth Lawrence. They moved to the polygamist enclave in Colorado City, Arizona and joined Eliot's other three wives and fifteen children. Mary Beth was taught that the woman's job is to serve God first and men second. Her mother modeled this for her by obeying Eliot Lawrence's every wish, and so when Mary Beth's stepbrothers started spying on her in the shower, poking her with sticks and pulling down her underpants, Mary Beth didn't object. She let them do what they wanted because she was a good girl, a pious girl and she didn't want to cause any trouble.

At thirteen, just two months after her period began and she had officially become a woman, Mary Beth was summoned for a meeting with the town Elder, Uncle Roy. He was seventy-eight years old, had thirty-nine wives and eighty-two children. God had spoken directly to Uncle Roy the night before and He said that Mary Beth was to become Uncle Roy's fortieth wife. She would bear him many children. Mary Beth did what any good Fundamentalist Latter Day Saint would do—the only thing she could do—in an impossible situation: she threw herself off the roof of her two story house, three days before the wedding, in hopes of meeting up with the Holy Father sooner rather than later and ending this hopeless life on earth. Unfortunately, she landed on her mother's well-tended hedge. Instead of heavenly grace she awoke to a broken wrist, collarbone and left leg. The marriage was called off but Mary Beth paid a price. Eliot Lawrence was humiliated by his wayward daughter. He and his sons took to beating Mary Beth almost on a daily basis, sometimes alone and sometimes in groups of two or three.

Mary Beth suffered her beatings in silence. God was punishing her for her selfish ways and she deserved it. And it wasn't always terrible. Sometimes, when just John William beat her, the eldest, most handsome and gentlest of her stepbrothers, Mary Beth almost enjoyed the pain and attention.

On Mary Beth's fifteenth birthday, Eliot Lawrence himself received a direct message from God: Mary Beth, his stepdaughter, was now ready to become Mary Beth his wife. The Lord said she would bear him many children and live in harmony with his other wives and children. He came to Mary Beth late one night, crawled into her bed and ran his hands up and down her body as he outlined their future together.

The next morning Mary Beth got up before dawn, slipped out of the house and ran into town. She didn't have a plan when she rounded the corner and saw the bakery truck parked in front of the market. The back of the truck was open and there was no one in sight. Mary Beth hid herself behind the racks of breads and pastries and rode out of Colorado City accompanied by the delicious smell of fresh-baked goods.

~

JACK BELMONT
DRIVER OF THE BAKERY TRUCK

She sure as hell didn't look that young, so I believed it when she said eighteen. I opened my truck and there she was all curled up behind the sourdough, looking scared in her weird old lady Mormon clothes. Didn't take a genius to figure the whole thing out. Girls run away from that place all the time. That's why they try to give the delivery jobs to their own kind—so the little chicas can't get far. It's a pretty sick town, all those young girls having babies with their daddies and their cousins and uncles. Place gives me the creeps. I was called in last minute that day, regular driver down with the flu. I'm telling you, I was the first lucky thing that ever happened in that girl's life.

She was pretty. Real fresh. Blond hair, clear blue eyes, kinda skinny in that way girls get just before they blossom. Her body drove me crazy. But the kid had a lot of damage. You gotta go slow. We holded up in my apartment for weeks and after a month together we were having the time of our lives.

Of course they came looking for her, that's how I found out she was fifteen, but no way was I sending her back. Maybe you think it was sick that I, a thirty-year-old man, had a little girl that age but, believe me, the alternative for her was much worse. We stayed inside mostly, kept the blinds drawn but you can't keep a girl locked up forever. After a couple of months we loaded up my truck and headed out.

We decided her name should be Honey. Hell, that's what I called her all the time anyway. Honey Belmont. No, we never got married, that's not my thing, but I didn't mind her using my name. We moved around a lot. Few weeks here, couple months there. I picked up odd jobs. Honey mostly hung out waiting for me.

It was good. And it stayed good for a couple years. Girl really knew how to take care of me. I think I loved her, or the closest I've ever come to love. But then she got pregnant. I don't know. I couldn't handle it. Changed everything. Some people just aren't cut out to be parents. The responsibility, all that crying, day and night, it made me mean. It was like they were asking for something I just didn't have to give and the more she and the baby needed, the more inadequate I felt. I was trapped and I said some things I should never have said. I hurt Honey with my words and I was afraid, if I stuck around, that it might get physical. So I left. She had a job waiting tables by then. I paid six months rent on the apartment and bailed. I'm not proud of what I've done. But hey, if it weren't for me, she'd still be in Colorado City so really, in a lot of ways, I did her a favor. She's much better off wherever she is.

28

Honey All Alone

The big question, the one that rattled Honey's brain night and day, was: what if Jack came back? What if Honey was working on Gus in the living room and Jack walked through the door? How would Jack feel if he saw her bent over the kitchen table and Gus pounding away, shouting out his dirty little string of swear words? Would it bother Jack to see her bottom spanked with a fly swatter? Her nipples smeared with honey? What if Jack changed his mind and came back to reclaim his little family and then ran into fat old Gus? He'd split. He'd call her a whore—which she was—then turn around and leave for good.

Honey wrestled the sheets off the bed. These were the Gus sheets and the Gus mattress cover. She only used them when he came over. Once he finished his business and was gone, she would pull them off the bed and wash them in the hottest water possible.

Why Gus? He wasn't exactly a choice she made. She didn't wake up one morning and say, "Gee, life is pretty tough. I'm a single mom barely making rent and Kimmy needs new shoes. Hmmm. I think I'll pick up some rich old guy who I can have sex with in return for extra money." She didn't suddenly feel homesick for the perverted old men, those nasty polygamists, of her youth. She was absolutely not looking for a father figure to torment her days and nights. No. Honey Belmont had been minding her own business, taking care not to think too far into the future, when Gus showed up at the restaurant where she worked. He came and sat in her section, day after day, and asked questions. At the end of a month he'd sucked out most of her past and all of her present, rendering her hollow and more vulnerable than ever before. The next thing Honey knew, Gus was paying her rent, buying groceries and taking care of Kimmy's preschool. And in exchange for these things, Honey let him paw her body with his old stubby-fat fingers. She lay beneath him while he drove himself deeper and deeper inside her, grunting and groaning and sweating away. His liver-lips kissed her. His bulging fisheyes memorized the area between her legs.

STOP

Honey took a deep breath and shook the pillow into the clean case. Gus was a wonderful, generous man. She put the pillow down and pulled the bedspread up. Gus Wentworth had arrived in her life just in the nick of time. Without him there probably would be no apartment. She was lucky to have a man like Gus. He was their ticket to a place to live, clothes, maybe even a car someday. Gus was very unhappy in his marriage. Gus' wife was skinny and harsh and that's why he preferred Honey's sweetness. If she could just make him happy enough, maybe he'd leave his wife and maybe Honey and Kimmy would finally have a future.

29

Norman's Thoughts on Love

Coyotes, prairie voles, sandhill cranes, beavers, termites, black vultures, barn owls and French angel fish are several examples of animals who mate for life. These creatures commit and never look back. It doesn't mean that they won't occasionally copulate with additional partners, just that they will stand by each other until one of the pair is killed or dies of natural causes.

Some males in the animal kingdom prefer to have more than one mate. These robust fellows are called polygynists and often travel with a large harem. But Mother Nature is fair and so, in many other species, you will find that it is the female who choses to have more than one mate, sometimes as many as fifty. These energetic gals are referred to as polyandrists and my hat goes off to them.

There are a few animals that are thought to be completely monogamous: swans, otters, bats, marmosets. One species of penguin performs an elaborate ritual when pledging a lifetime commitment. The male selects a female for "marriage" out of a vast population of thousands. He presents her with a small stone, which he places at her feet. If she accepts the gift, they stand belly to belly and sing a mating song. After a two-week "getting-to-know-you" period, the male will make his amorous intentions known by laying his head across his beloved's stomach. The two lovebirds will then head out across the ice to find a cozy spot where they can consummate their union in private.

There are all sorts of choices for our furry and feathered friends, but it has been proven that monogamy amongst a species heightens the odds of extinction. Just so you know.

30

Time to Pick up Kimmy

Honey sat on the little bench by the sandbox and busied herself with the yellow plastic shovel and bucket. She could hear the kids inside singing the cleanup song. Honey was early. Early was better than late because she didn't have to pay a penalty but early meant she had to wait with the other Happy Helper parents and guardians. Some days she'd rather pay.

The maids stood over in the corner by the slide. They wore nice pants and blouses or designer sweat suits. These women spoke perfect English. They drove their employers' fancy cars, cooked fancy meals and read to the children. They had health insurance and dental plans. They carried nice purses, kept their hands well manicured and had an arrogance that made Honey want to run away and hide. They would stare at her dirty sneakers and then look away in disgust. Honey wanted to shout, "Hey, you're just maids." But the truth was, these women had it far more together than she did. They had climbed a steep slope and were now standing at the top of the mountain. She was still at the bottom, looking up, searching for the trailhead. Honey knew that if she applied in one of those fancy households for the lowly job of housekeeper, she would be sent away. She was simply not qualified.

On the other side of the waiting area stood the stay-at-home moms. Honey had hoped that she would find a friend or two in this group. She envisioned long giggly lunches or hurried whispered coffees. She imagined a network of supportive women who would offer her advice and understanding. Honey longed for someone to confide in. But Honey was out of luck. These women would smile when she said hello, but then they turned their backs and resumed their conversations and Honey was invariably left standing all alone.

The red door opened and the children came spilling out, happy faces and cute little outfits. Kimmy was at the back of the group with Miss Angela. She had a cold. Honey had given her double the recommended dosage of Dimetapp early this morning and her sinuses seemed to dry up but now Honey saw that the medicine had worn off. Kimmy's nose was running, thick and yellow. Honey stood up and took a deep breath. Miss Angela was holding Kimmy's arm and coming her way. She did not look happy.

"Kimmy curled up in the quiet corner and slept through most of the morning session." Miss Angela didn't bother with a greeting. She stood right in Honey's face and delivered her message loud and clear, almost as if she wanted the others to hear. "When she woke up, she was extremely congested. Look at the mucous!"

"I'm sorry." Honey couldn't think of anything else. She was sorry.

"Kimmy told us that she didn't want to come this morning." Miss Angela raised her voice in case those over by the gate were having trouble hearing. "She said she told you she was sick. She said she begged."

It was true. Kimmy had begged not to come this morning. But Kimmy begged every morning. Kimmy hated this school. She said that the kids never played with her and that the teachers were mean. Honey would have liked to put her at another preschool but Happy Helpers was within walking distance of the apartment and until she got a car, this was the only option.

"I'm really sorry," Honey said. She put her arm around Kimmy's shoulders. "I didn't think she was that sick."

"We have policies." Now Miss Angela angled her body slightly away from Honey so as to make a general announcement. "Yellow or green mucus stays home. Clear is fine. A child must be fever-free for twenty-four hours, minimum, before returning. No vomiting or diarrhea. Rashes, pinkeye, cold sores on the lips or in the mouth—these are all things that are to be taken care of in the home. They do not belong here at school."

"I know." Honey pulled Kimmy close. "I'm so sorry. I'll take her home. It won't happen again."

"No, it won't." Miss Angela put her hand on Honey's shoulder to stop her from leaving. "You've repeatedly been late at pickup. You've completely disregarded the school's policy of recyclable lunch containers by sending Kimmy to school with those prepackaged snacks. The snacks themselves violate the healthy-food-only policy and have caused a lot of trouble with the other children. Kimmy sneaks candy. I've even caught her with gum. We've discussed this, do you remember?"

Honey nodded her head.

Angela went on. "This is not the first cold that Kimmy's brought to school. Kimmy seems to be sick a lot. Personally, I think it might have something to do with diet and the fact that she never seems to have a jacket or a sweater."

"She has a sweater," Honey said. "And a jacket."

"Whatever." Angela folded her arms across her chest. "My point is, I don't think that Happy Helpers is the right place for Kimmy. I just don't think that our school is a good fit for your family."

"No, it fits fine," Honey said.

"I'm afraid we're going to have to ask you not to come back."

"I won't send her to school sick anymore, I promise," Honey said.

"I'm sorry."

"But we paid."

"We'll refund the difference."

"There aren't any other schools around here." Honey was afraid she might start to cry. "We have no where else to go."

"Nothing I can do about that." Miss Angela turned to go back into the school.

"Please."

"Good luck to you," Miss Angela said as she closed the red door.

Kimmy wanted to be carried. She had a headache and Honey thought probably a fever. They needed a thermometer at home, why couldn't Honey ever remember to buy one? Thermometer and children's Tylenol. Honey picked up Kimmy. She was a skinny girl, barely forty pounds, and it was true that she was sick a lot. It was hard to get her to eat anything other than chips and hot dogs. What was Honey supposed do? Force-feed her spinach? Truth was, Honey didn't really care for fruits and vegetables either. She'd buy some grapes. Grapes were good and Kimmy would eat them if they were frozen.

"My angel," Honey said. "We'll walk to the market and get you some medicine. Then we'll go home."

"They don't want us, huh Mommy?" Kimmy rested her head on Honey's shoulder.

"No, baby. They don't."

"It's okay." Kimmy shifted her weight. "I'll stay home with you."

Honey walked down the street towards the market. What was she going to do? Who would take care of Kimmy while she was at work? What about when Gus came over? Honey didn't even know where to begin to look for her answers.

31

Gus to the Rescue

*I*f Gus had been busy, if he'd had something, anything, to do that afternoon, if he hadn't already gassed up the car and had it washed and the tires filled with air, if there weren't still another three hours to kill before dinner at the country club, he probably would have ignored Honey's cry for help. He probably would have put it off and maybe made a phone call the next day. He might have sent a letter. He probably would have done so anonymously. But Gus really didn't have anything better to do on that afternoon and so he drove to the Happy Helpers Preschool. He parked the Bentley in the *Loading and Unloading Only* zone and walked up to the bright red door.

Gus had never been here, of course. He'd only seen Kimmy that first time when he visited the apartment. Kid looked like something off a famine poster from the depths of poorest Africa, ribcage, cheekbones, bulging eyes and all. Except, of course, Kimmy was white. She didn't say much but she stared at Gus with that awful hunger that made him want to lock her up in a closet. When Honey told him she couldn't afford the local preschool and so Kimmy had to stay home—Gus had written a check.

The knob on the red door was high, eye level. Gus assumed

that was to keep the kids from escaping. He tried but it was locked. Shit. What if they were gone for the day? He didn't even know the name of this god damn place. Gus pounded. He could hear someone moving around inside. What the fuck was he doing here? This wasn't his job. He'd never even stepped foot in a school when his children were young. That was Judith's territory. Women's work. Hell, he had no idea where his grandchildren went or even what grade they were in. He waited but no one came. Gus put his ear to the door; it sounded like someone was sweeping.

He knocked again, this time using his key. It scratched the paint but made a much louder noise. "Hello? Are you there?" Why was he doing this?

Gus listened. The sweeping had stopped.

"HELLO." Gus pounded then put his ear to the door and heard the sweeping resume.

"Hey." Gus rattled the handle. "Come on." He kicked the door but it hurt his toe so he turned around and used his heel, which was hard and sharp. BANG, BANG, BANG. "Open up, goddamn it." His heel actually chipped some of the red paint off the door and you could see the gray primer coat. He felt strong, kicking that door. Nothing could stop August Wentworth. He felt like he could break the damn thing down if he wanted to. A young buck, a strapping young man, still lived in this old body. Gus looked back; there were little divots in the wood. How deep he could make those divots, how much paint could he chip off? Let's show these motherfuckers something. Gus Wentworth was not to be ignored. He switched legs and started in with his left foot just as the door was flung opened. Gus stumbled backwards a couple of steps but caught himself before he fell.

"What the fuck is going on?" the woman said.

Gus whirled around. She was hard and pointy like a pair of needle-nose pliers. Her hair was straight and cut at a sharp angle just at the chin. Judith wore her hair that way. Was that why this woman looked so familiar?

"Mr. Wentworth?"

Shit. How the hell did she know his name?

"Angela Simms." She held out her hand and laughed. "I had dinner at your house a couple of nights ago. With Conrad. Remember?"

"Of course. What a coincidence." Gus shook then put his hands in his pockets and searched furiously for a plan. "So this is your school?"

"Everything all right?" she said.

This was not good. He saw her glance at the battered door then back up to his face. She kept that fake smile, a strangely Judith-like smile, plastered across her face. This girl was trouble.

"Fine," Gus cleared his throat. "I'm here to discuss a student who attends your school. Or did. Did attend your school."

"Who?"

"Honey Belmont."

Angela Simms studied his face. That toxic smile.

"I mean, Kimmy. Kimmy Belmont." Gus laughed at his mistake. He hoped he sounded good-natured and casual. "Kimmy's the daughter, Honey's the mother. Of course."

Angela smiled. "Come in," she said.

As she took his arm and lead him through the door Gus felt like he was being sucked into a swirling vortex of doom.

———

Honey Belmont was the last thing that Angela expected from August Wentworth. The little slut. She was an ignorant Utah farm girl, plain and utterly stupid, probably hadn't made it past the seventh grade. But one should never underestimate white trash. They were the vermin of our society, impossible to exterminate. Beverly Hills was crawling with rats and cockroaches. Still, Angela couldn't even begin to figure out how Honey had pulled it off. A Wentworth?

Why had Angela ever admitted her to the school? Stupid mistake. But it seemed like the right thing at the time. Something about the challenge of fixing damaged goods and the fact that Angela tried for some semblance of diversity at the school. Nowadays you couldn't just have rich white kids at your school, it was actually a law, and so right from the start Angela had made a point of reaching out to families of color. People liked the idea of diversity. There were the Washingtons with their adorable twin boys, black as midnight. The Yamamotos were a lovely family, so quiet and clean. Little Camilla Rodriguez had an Argentinean father. But Angela didn't have any underprivilegeds. So when Honey showed up and wanted to enroll—and she was actually able to pay the tuition (a mystery, now solved)—Angela thought it would bring some sort of good pre-school karma if she admitted a little white trash. She had visions of changing the child's life with lessons in hygiene and elocution. Perhaps Kimmy would read early as a result of Angela's attention. Maybe there was some sort of artistic potential that she could nur-ture. Angela could help the mother too with personal presentation and poise. But Honey and Kimmy were not good students. Kimmy was apathetic, uninterested in the most basic of activities. She was a child completely devoid of a personality. And Honey seemed to have some sort of attention deficit or learning disability; she never quite seemed to be all there. After a month, Angela realized it was hope-less so she gave up. Kimmy blended into the scenery, most of the children and staff ignored her, and Angela turned her attention else-where. The Belmonts fell off Angela's radar—they didn't cause any trouble, not really—until that terrible head-lice episode when 90 percent of the students were infested and a couple of the teachers too. A total nightmare. Of course Angela couldn't prove it, but she knew where those first nits came from. She could just imagine that filthy Belmont apartment. It was a relief to finally get rid of them.

And yet, here was August Wentworth asking for a favor.

Gus told Angela the truth about how he met Honey at that diner on Wilshire. He said they'd become friends. He talked about her unfortunate circumstances and the importance of charity. He confessed that he had a real soft spot for sweet little Kimmy. He told her about how he'd mentored lots of kids through the years and lately he'd assumed the "grandfather" role in the Belmonts' lives. He was very concerned with Kimmy's education. She was a bright kid, definitely going places. Kimmy Belmont was special and she deserved another chance.

Angela listened carefully, nodded and smiled at all the right places, crossed her legs, folded her hands in intense concentration. But when he finished his story, it was clear that she didn't believe a word of it. He could see that she knew instinctively what this was really about. He could practically hear her brain working behind those cold eyes. What was in it for her? How could she take Gus Wentworth's sordid affair and turn it into a jackpot? She had him balanced on a blue plastic nursery school chair, his big body spilling over the sides, his knees pushing up against his chest, waiting for her verdict.

It wasn't that Gus worried about his reputation. And he wasn't too worried about Judith. Judith believed pretty much anything he told her and would in fact fight to the death to defend him if a scandal should arise. No, what bothered Gus was that he was wasting his afternoon in a damn preschool, squatting on doll's furniture, pleading with this skinny-assed witch. Gus hated to ask for favors. It undermined his position of power. Gus made a point never to owe anyone anything but this lollipop would have something on him when she said yes and then he'd feel compromised. His standards had been lowered. He'd allowed himself to be drawn into something that was beneath him. What did he care where Honey's kid went to school? What did he really care about Honey? She was just another one in a long string of women, wasn't she?

"So?" Gus put his hands on his thighs and pushed himself up into a standing position. His knees cracked and his back seized on him but he was careful not to grimace. "What do you say, Angela? Do you have a place for Kimmy?"

"Of course." Angela stood. "I'm so glad you came today, August. I just didn't understand what was going on but now that I

know I'll do everything I can to help. You can count on me."
Angela leaned in and gave Gus a hug. "I think we're going to be
good friends, you and I."

Gus patted her shoulder and headed for the door. At any
minute now her incisors would elongate.

"You tell Honey that she and Kimmy are more than welcome
at Happy Helpers." Angela opened the red door to let him out.

"I'll do that." Gus resisted the urge to run as he walked
through the door. "Thank you."

"And I'll expect to see more of you," Angela said from the
doorway. "Now that we're friends."

Gus waved his hand in what he hoped was a friendly farewell
then picked up pace as he rushed to his car.

32

The Wentworths Take
Maggie Haliburton to Dinner

*J*udith never really liked Maggie Halliburton, truth be told. Maggie was humorless, dull, and in Judith's humble opinion, more than a little bit stupid. Sure, she followed the conversation, laughed at the appropriate moments. She clapped her hands and yelled bravo or shed tears of sympathy when called upon. If you weren't paying attention, you'd probably think she was a contributor, a fun dinner partner, a very good friend. But if you listened closely, as Judith did, you'd notice that Maggie simply collected and repackaged the thoughts of her friends then re-presented them with a confident pat on the shoulder and a big "don't you think?" Of course that's what they thought, they'd just said so a half hour ago. It was so irritating and yet so effective. No one ever seemed to catch on. And all the men were crazy about her. Maggie was the most beautiful in their group of friends. She was the one that they had courted in high school and college, long before Judith came on the scene. Beautiful and from a very rich, old Los Angeles family. But all the good looks and money in the world couldn't hide the fact that Maggie was a simpleton who got by on her courtesan charms. Why, you could still find Maggie resting her hand on the knee of an attractive dinner partner with just a tad too much familiarity. Maggie, who kissed all handsome men on the lips, was still a flirt at 65. Imagine, at that age. No, Judith was not fond of that woman. She had tolerated her for August's sake and, of course, because of that adorable husband David, but if she was honest with herself she'd have to admit that she positively loathed Maggie Halliburton.

And now David was dead after a long and ugly struggle with lung cancer. David was dead and Maggie was devastated and it was Judith's job to play nursemaid. Why did it always have to fall to the wives? Why couldn't August be the one holding Maggie's hand? They'd known each other since nursery school, for God's sake. And yet, Judith wouldn't really want August performing that task. Who knows what kind of stunt Maggie would pull if given the chance?

Judith had made the call. *"Dear one, this is a difficult time, and I know that you just want to curl up in a ball and hide away from the world but you simply must come out with us. It will be good for you, for all of us. We love you and you know how much everyone misses David. Thursday night, the country club. I won't take no for an answer."* Or something along those lines. Judith didn't even know what she'd said. She just opened her mouth and let the falsehoods spill forth and of course Maggie had agreed. Even in her darkest hour, Maggie wouldn't dream of missing a dinner date and a chance to flirt with someone else's husband.

Gus wasn't home yet. If he didn't get back soon, they would be late. Judith tried him in the car again but there was no answer. Where could he be? Gus was either at the club playing golf or dominoes or poker with the same men he'd been playing with since he was a small boy, or he was home taking a nap. But he'd left the club hours ago. Gus didn't do things or go places by himself. He needed people around him, family and friends and he was a creature of habit. It wasn't like Gus to be late. Where could he be?

Judith needed to finish applying the subtle bit of make-up she wore and then she'd concentrate on finding her husband. She leaned into the mirror and brushed on her mascara. Women her age and older needed to be careful not to over-paint; it was a common mistake. Fools thought that if they just pile on more foundation, brighter lipstick and darker brows, no one will notice how their faces are falling off their skulls. Tonight the club would be packed full of clown-like matrons with withered mouths and wattled necks. So many of them chose not to fix what was so easily taken care of. Why didn't they just have face-lifts like Judith? Why weren't they more concerned about their appearance? And why for God sake didn't they watch their weight? The Los Angeles Country Club was filled with WASPy rich cows who started to drop the reins on their appearance around the age of forty and let nature take over by the time they hit their mid-fifties, just as their mothers and grandmothers had before them. Barbara Bush on parade. It was some sort of reverse snobbery that Judith had never understood. "I'm fat and gray and starting to look like an old man, but it doesn't matter because I am of superior stock and needn't concern myself with silly things like appearance." Well, they could have it. Judith was not buying in. Never. She'd watch what she ate and keep seeing Dr. Graulich whenever she needed a little tightening. Judith planned to leave this earth in a stunning package. Obviously Maggie Halliburton felt the same way.

August walked into the bedroom and threw himself on the bed.

"Where on earth have you been?" Judith said. She sat next to him and kissed his cheek. He smelled of that awful lotion the masseuse used at the club. Vanilla? Strawberry? Why couldn't they invest in a finer line of products? Perhaps Judith should take matters into her own hands and send August off with a big bottle of unscented oil. Yes, that's what she would do. Tomorrow.

"I've been out and about." He rolled over and put a pillow over his head.

"August, you need a shower," she said. "We've got to leave in ten minutes or we'll be late."

"I just need a second." He curled into a ball as if he were set-tling in for a long nap.

Judith took the pillow off his head. "Did you get my message about the tongs?" she said.

He looked at her, confused. Sometimes he could be so dense.

"No, never mind," Judith said. "We'll talk about it later. Get up. Hurry. We mustn't be late."

Judith brought August up to date on the tongs as they drove to the club. She started at the beginning with her breakfast in the courtyard and how the breakfast tray had come and she immedi-ately noticed they were missing. She went into detail about inter-viewing the maids and how she'd called each of the children. It was so frustrating, no one had a clue and frankly, no one seemed to really care. August drove the car but he didn't appear to be listen-ing. Where did that man go? Honestly, sometimes he seemed like he was on another planet. Judith wondered if maybe she should schedule him a physical, just to make sure everything was all right. You couldn't be too careful, at their age. She reached over and gave his arm a little shake. "Are you listening to me, August?"

"Of course," he said. "The tongs. Go on."

So she continued but when she'd finished the story, all he had to say was, "I'm sure they'll turn up." And that did not make Judith feel any better. Those tongs would not just "turn up" on their own. No, Judith would have to make them turn up. It would be nice to have a little support once in a while. Afterall, they were August's tongs too.

Judith took a deep breath, flipped down the visor and checked her lipstick in the vanity mirror. She would not let this ruin her evening. August turned the car into the club's driveway and Judith patted his hand. "We're going to have a nice evening," she announced.

August nodded his head but did not answer. Judith wondered if he was coming down with something. He seemed so distant. She watched as he got out of the car, walked around to open her door.

He looked fine. She smiled at him and he smiled back so she took his arm and together they strolled into the clubhouse.

Lewis the ancient, charcoal, maitre'd bowed as they mounted the steps to the dining room. He'd been wasting away for years but the club never thought to buy him a new tuxedo and so now it hung from his shoulders and puddled on his shoes.

"Good evening Mr. Wentworth, Missus Wentworth."

"Lewis." August slapped him on the back with what Judith considered a bit too much force but Lewis stood his ground.

The dining room was nearly full. Judith loved this room. It was right out of one of her girlhood fantasies. High vaulted ceiling with four huge crystal chandeliers, the far wall of the room was all windows with gigantic French doors that opened on a magnificent terrace. The golf course spread out in every direction and from this room you would never know you were in the middle of Beverly Hills. It was a magical oasis.

Lewis gathered the menus. "Right this way."

Judith and August weren't able to keep up with Lewis. There were people at every table who had to be addressed. August had belonged here all his life and there weren't many members he didn't know. Plus Thursday night was the seafood buffet, very popular. You could always count on seeing those whom you cared about on Thursdays. Judith kissed the ladies and hugged the men and she felt entirely happy and secure as she sat down. These were her friends, her peers, her people. She let her eyes scan the room. Was there anyone she missed? They'd said hello to the Schwinns, the Carters, the McManns, and the Adamsons. She waved to the Gillettes. Then her eyes landed on that awful Charles Worthington. Why he was still a member here, Judith could not understand. Such a creepy man and there'd been that run-in with the law, something about muscle-bound prostitutes and drugs and hidden cameras. Of course he was acquitted, with that kind of money who wouldn't be, but there was no question of his guilt. Honestly, his membership should have been revoked but the Worthingtons were one of the original families and there was something in the bylaws that stopped the board of directors from expelling the wretched man. Talk about a black sheep. He never socialized with the other members. He just came in, several nights a week, and ate his meals alone at the table in the far corner by the kitchen, then left. Judith turned her chair away and put him out of her mind. She was determined to enjoy this evening.

Judith ordered a glass of champagne and August asked for a double scotch and soda. When Pedro, the waiter, walked away Judith said, "Double scotches are not part of our agreement."

"Put a cork in it, Judith," August cleared his throat. "I had a rough day."

"What, you lost at dominoes?"

August glared at Judith with all the built-up anger of forty years of marriage. Then he started cracking the knuckles on his left hand, a habit that she found absolutely revolting. Judith smoothed the napkin over her lap. She needed to get a hold of herself. What was she thinking, starting a fight here at the club? Maggie was due to arrive any minute.

"I'm sorry, darling." She took his right hand, before he could start cracking it, and squeezed. "I guess we're all a little shaken up. David's death and all. Forgive me?"

He extracted his hand from hers and set to work on the cuticles. This man was such a child. Were any of their friends watching? Judith scanned the room. All seemed to be engaged in conversation.

Judith started over. "Tell me about today, sweetheart."

August dropped his hands and straightened his spine. "What do you mean?"

"You said you had a rough day," Judith said. What was that look on his face? "You all right, August?"

Just then Maggie arrived. She wore a turtleneck under a slim fitted jacket and a tight skirt with kick pleats. All black. Very flattering. The stylish, beautiful widow, Maggie Halliburton brave, stunning and all alone to the world. August stood to welcome her even though Maggie was all the way across the room. It would take her awhile to reach them because she would stop at each of the tables to receive condolences. Judith watched as the husbands gave long, warm hugs while most of the wives looked on with false sympathy. Beautiful widows were not particularly welcome amongst the married women here. Once your husband died you were cast out of the inner circle, especially if you posed a threat. Judith suspected that Maggie didn't have any real friends in this room and that soon she would stop coming to the club altogether as did most of the widows. Maggie was never much of a golfer so there really wouldn't be much of a point to her hanging around. No, it wouldn't be long before they were asking each other how Maggie was and no one would really know.

When she finally got close to their table, Judith jumped up and threw her arms around Maggie before August could move in. "Darling, darling, darling." Judith held her tight and rocked her back and forth. "I'm so glad you're here." Maggie hugged back with surprising passion and her body shuddered with a sob.

"Come on," Judith said. "Sit down, let me get you a drink." And Judith helped Maggie into a chair thus depriving August of the chance to physically show his support.

——

When Gus looked at Maggie he still saw that seventeen-year-old girl with the clear, clear brown eyes and the brilliant smile. She was frozen there in time for him, so full of life and possibilities. Part of his brain registered the fact that Maggie's skin was papery now, thin and vulnerable. Her lips were no longer full in the way they'd been in high school and her hair was not that same deep lustrous brown. But as he reached across the table to take her hand, it was the Maggie of his boyhood, the beautiful Maggie of his young dreams whom he sought to comfort. He had always loved this girl and part of him always would.

"How you holding up?" Gus took her hand.

"She is holding up just fine." Judith took Maggie's other hand. "Aren't you, Maggie?"

Sometimes Gus wished that Judith would just evaporate. A little puff of wind and she'd be gone. His wife's whining voice and constant nagging tore at him over the years, physically, and now she was like the chronic but not quite lethal ailments that he suffered on a daily basis. Judith was his arthritic hip, his achy low back, his very painful tennis elbow. There was no cure for Judith, just pain medication and a stiff upper lip.

"I'm going to be fine," Maggie said. She withdrew her hands and put them in her lap. "Thank you both for inviting me. I don't seem to want to leave the house very much. I don't want to do much of anything except sleep, but I know that will change. Eventually. I'll be fine."

That's what Gus liked about Maggie, she was straightforward. Ask her a question and she'd give you an honest answer. No drama, no silliness.

It was awful, David dying. He was too young, wasn't he? Wasn't this too soon? It seemed very unfair to Gus, and it scared him that his group of friends, these lifetime companions, were entering that final stage where memories became the focal point and the future no longer seemed so sure. He wanted to hug Maggie and tell her he'd always loved her. He wanted to cry with her over David's death but instead took a good long pull on his scotch and let his thoughts drift to more immediate problems while Judith took over the conversation.

33

A Reflective Moment with Norman

*M*y parents: August and Judith, Incubus and Succubus. He rapes and pillages while she sucks the life and humor out of all who enter her realm. They are a perfect match, made in hell. When I close my eyes I see August with his tongue lolling out of his mouth, chin wet with spit and mucous, eyes bloodshot with lust and rage. His hunger is all consuming. He is a feverish creature who can never be satisfied. And over there, crouched in the corner, is Judith with her pinched narrow face and her single row of teeth waiting, like a spider, to drain the joy from any being who tragically stumbles into her web. An evening with Judith will render you gray, devoid of color. You will feel very cold after just a few moments in her presence. She will steal and destroy any hope or dream that you hold close and leave you devastated, filled with despair. They will stay together for all eternity, my parents. Avoid them and their offspring at all costs.

I am immune, vaccinated by right of birth. I am only here for a few more moments, treading water, awaiting my next instruction. It is long overdue, no question, but it's coming and I will be ready when it comes. My antenna is up, receivers switched on, full volume and I'm at the controls. Any minute now, I'll be gone and you'll be left on your own. Don't say I didn't warn you.

34

Paul Springs into Action

Paul knew, in his heart of hearts he knew, that his son had a problem. Something was not right with this boy, and his attempts at conversation, man to man, had been a complete failure. The kid was withdrawn and sullen. Paul had gone to the library and done a lot of research. Joey was definitely exhibiting some troubling symptoms: the secrecy, the locked doors, the withdrawn behavior. Paul had to get to the bottom of this, and if his son was a drug addict, well, he'd deal with it. After careful reading, Paul realized that both Joey and Monica were at risk, genetically at risk. Look at Uncle Norman, clearly he had substance abuse issues. Grandpa August was an alcoholic who hid his addiction behind an extreme enthusiasm for collecting wine. And unfortunately it looked like Becky might be developing a problem with sleeping pills and possibly anti-anxiety medications. So yes, his wife and children had a little defective DNA but it was nothing he couldn't handle. These things could be solved with early detection and intervention. There were steps he could take and a whole army of people out there who could help if needed. But the first thing he had to do was determine exactly the extent of the problem. There was only one solution — a thorough search of the premises.

Paul walked into Little Joey's room and closed the door. The kids were at school and Becky was off at one of her exercise classes but Paul didn't particularly want Lucy, the housekeeper, to know what he was up to. This was a Wentworth-Jones issue, a private family matter, and so he locked the door behind him. The bed was made, neatly as before. That in itself told Paul that something was wrong. Little Joey, the slob, was suddenly making an effort to take care of his room? No, Little Joey had obviously instigated a cover-up. Paul knelt by the bed and checked the hole in the mattress. He didn't expect to find anything but it was the easiest place to start. Nothing. Then removed the covers and pulled the mattress off the box springs. Bingo. There, towards the middle of the box spring, lay a small green canvas pencil pouch, the kind that kids used at school. The momentary thrill of discovery was instantly replaced by fear as Paul sat on the bed. He knew it, Paul had always felt he had better than average instincts and here again was proof of that fact. His son was in trouble. His son needed help. Paul took a deep breath and reached for the pouch. He would do whatever it took to make things right. Joey was young; they were catching this thing early. Paul slowly opened the zipper and told himself that no matter what he found, he could deal with it. They would all work together and get counseling, as a family.

Paul dumped the contents of the pouch on the bed and stared. A set of nudie playing cards, a pen with a women in a disappearing swimsuit (depending which way you held the pen), a plastic minia-ture female doll with a strong resemblance to Helen Hunt that was anatomically correct complete with pubic hair, a cheap belt buckle that spelled F-U-C-K, an extra large flavored condom and a small aerosol spray labeled *Pussy in a Can.* He actually laughed out loud. This was Little Joey's big secret? Paul picked up the pen and drained the swimsuit halfway so the woman was topless. This was the healthy collection of a normal heterosexual boy and Paul almost felt proud. He sprayed a little of the pussy scent into the air; it actually smelled like a woman. What kid wouldn't want this stuff? Good for Joey, and it would be *Joey* from now on. He wasn't

Little anymore, he was becoming a young man and the family needed to treat him as such. Paul was happy and relieved as he reloaded the boyish treasures, replaced the pouch and reassembled the bed. There was nothing wrong with his son, he was just growing up.

The room looked just as it had when he entered and Paul was about to leave when he decided he should look around a little more, get to know his son better, double check that there wasn't anything else going on. He went to the shelves and pulled out a couple of random books, checking for hollowed out secret compartments. He'd once seen a movie where the bad drug dealers taped their stashes to the back of the toilet and so, just for fun, he looked there. He cleared out the towels and searched under the sink. Nothing. Then he walked into the closet and opened the drawers. T-shirts, underwear, socks. Boy stuff. An ordinary closet. Paul was going to leave when he spotted a neon pink hippopotamus tucked away in the corner on the upper most top shelf. It was the kind of stuffed animal you might win at a carnival, ugly and very feminine with a lavender bow tied at its neck and huge plastic eyes. He reached up and pulled the thing down. It was heavy. Too heavy. What the hell was in this thing? Paul ran his fingers along the seams then flipped the animal over. Sure enough there was a split in the stomach that was held shut with tiny gold safety pins. He opened the seam and pulled out a Ziplock bag full of pennies, Becky's lost diamond earring wrapped in tissue paper, a set of old cuff links that Paul had misplaced years ago, a porcelain ashtray from the Treetops Hotel in Tanzania and a glass eye. Paul picked up the bag of pennies and checked the dates. 1907, 1919, 1923. His childhood collection here in a bag in Joey's closet.

Paul tore the room apart. He found hiding places everywhere. Joey had cut a hole in the drywall behind his shoe rack. He'd loosened a tile in the bathroom and hollowed out an area of the flooring. He had things stashed in the heating vents, the stereo, the television and even in the base of the humidifier. Paul turned that room upside down and when he was finished he was faced with a pile of stuff that made him dizzy with confusion. What was this thing he was dealing with? Why did Joey have three sets of Becky's keys, Paul's shoe horn, a toggle wrench, lipstick, golf balls, an engraved gold watch with the inscription *Conrad August Wentworth*, teaspoons and salt shakers, a framed picture of five Latin children standing outside a church somewhere in South America, necklaces and bracelets, knives, sun glasses, a yellowing set of dentures and Judith's antique silver tongs? What on earth did this kid need these things for? Why would he steal from all these people? Paul sat there on the floor of Joey's room and realized that his son was an absolute stranger.

35

Norman: Into the Wild

Have you ever killed anything? Watched the life force expire while you stood by holding the smoking gun? Did it thrill you? Give you the kind of release you'd always hope for in the bedroom? My father took me deer hunting in the Sierras when I was thirteen. One time only. Conrad had gone off to college and I think August was lonely in a house full of women. He was determined to make me into a man.

There were several months of preparation for the trip. I was taken to the skeet-shooting range every Saturday and encouraged to learn the ins and outs of annihilating the clay pigeons. During the week my father would come home early and the two of us would have target practice in the backyard with tin cans and a pellet gun. To everyone's surprise, I was a pretty good shot, better than Conrad when he was my age, and for a brief moment my father gave me his undivided attention.

At night, after dinner, August and I would retire to his study and close the door. He'd sit behind his desk and I'd perch on one of the ostrich skin sofas. I always sat on the edge, sure that any minute he'd lose interest in me and I would be asked to leave. But that never happened. He told me long stories about hunting in

Africa, the close calls, the incredible thrill of the hunt, the victory of the kill. I listened carefully and pushed down all feelings of revulsion. This was my big chance to have a relationship with my father.

There is a lot to learn about the killing of an animal and I was surprised by the complex ethical code that my father shared with other hunters. One must aim carefully, shot selection and placement is key. A good hunter never takes the "frontal" shot. The vulnerable area is too narrow and there's a good chance that you will wound but not kill the animal. Likewise with the "rear" shot, or the "Texas heart shot" as my father liked to call it.

"On a rear shot, you're not going to get a kill," August would say while sipping his port. "And no creature needs two assholes."

Ideally the deer would "quarter away" so that the angle of the shot would enter the body in a straight line aiming towards the opposite front leg. In a perfect world, your bullet would pass through both lungs but if you aimed a little farther forward you would have a good chance of getting the heart. Either way the animal would, in theory, die quickly and you would have exercised responsible sportsmanship. We talked about the challenges of selecting an animal in a herd, the importance of waiting for the exact right moment. He cautioned me to avoid moving shots and skyline shots. Never shoot through a barbed wire fence as it might deflect your bullet and always know what lies beyond before you fire your gun. It was a lot to take in but I paid close attention.

We headed out one weekend in early fall. I liked dressing in the warm camouflage jacket and matching pants even though they were too big for me. There was a guide, Phillip, someone whom my father knew well. We headed off into the trees, me being careful not to step on branches or trip over rocks—it was important to be absolutely silent. I had trouble keeping up.

Is your mouth watering? Are you thinking that I'm going to take you through the most traumatic incident of my life, step by step? The experience that will allow you to finally understand me? Perhaps you're anticipating tears and an overwhelming sense of sympathy? Empathy? Do you think that once I've recounted the details, you will be able to label and tuck me away into one of your neat cubbyholes?

Of course I didn't do it. I never fired a shot. There were many opportunities but each time I lowered my gun. Killing for survival made perfect sense to my young mind, but the pursuit of a trophy held no appeal. My father and the guide were patient with me at first but after awhile I became invisible as they went on with the hunt.

There's a picture from that trip of my father in the back of the pick-up truck, lifting the head of an enormous buck by the antlers, posing for the camera. He's smiling.

36

Father and Number One Son

*C*onrad crossed and then uncrossed his legs. Seven million things to take care of and fucking August is late for lunch. When would his father realize that other people had lives too? Conrad thought he would tell him. Today. He'd say: *Dad, I don't mind dropping everything and meeting you for lunch. I really don't. You're my father and you're a great father. But you have to realize that I'm a very busy guy and I can't spend my whole day waiting for you to show up at a restaurant. I've got clients, big case coming up. I'm an important man, Dad. You need to respect that.* No that wasn't right. That's not what he meant at all. What he needed to say was: *What the fuck? You think your time's more valuable than mine? You can just call me and drag me away? How about I start charging you by the hour? Fifteen bucks a minute, buddy, how's that sound?* Yeah, that's what he'd say. He'd tell the old man that next time he "had an important matter to discuss" he could either do it over the phone, with the meter running, or call Norman and his son-in-law Paul. Those two losers had all the time in the world.

Conrad looked up and saw that August had in fact arrived but was talking, flirting, with the chunky hostess by the entrance. The guy had no shame; if it was young and female then August

Wentworth had to make a play for it. Conrad smiled. He remembered when he was fourteen and August decided it was time for him to lose his virginity. Conrad had not been at all sure he liked the idea of his father orchestrating his initiation into manhood but August would not take no for an answer. They told Judith they were going to the movies, jumped in the car one Saturday afternoon and headed off to a whorehouse in Culver City. At that young age, Conrad had expected the place to look like something out of the old west, complete with saloon and petticoats but when they pulled up he saw that this was just an ordinary tract house set on a block alongside countless others. He had been somewhat disappointed until he went inside and met the young woman his father had picked out for him. Her name was Molly and she was beautiful, not much older than he. It made Conrad smile to think of her now with her sweet young face and body. He'd spent three hours in that little bedroom and would probably still be there today if his dad hadn't finally pulled him out.

"Hello, son." August lowered himself into the chair and signaled the waitress. His father would need to order and finish his habitual lunchtime martini before Conrad would even have a chance of finding out what this meeting was about. There was no doubt that there was a pressing issue, he could tell from the sound of his father's voice on the phone, but he knew that the ritual would have to be played out before they could get down to business. It seemed like there were few things left in August's life that brought him pleasure and these long, boozy lunches were high on the list. As the years passed, so too did August's interests. He'd let his membership at the fly-fishing club in Wyoming lapse. He hadn't been on a hunting trip in over four years. He didn't go to the skeet range anymore and in fact had mentioned, several times, that he might want to sell his gun collection.

"Drinking, Con?" August winked at the waitress.

"No Dad, I gotta work."

This was the man whom Conrad had idolized when he was a child. A man bigger than life. Stronger, funnier, wiser than any of the other dads.

"I'll have a Bombay martini," August told the waitress. "Very dirty, with four olives." August chuckled, apparently delighted by the mere thought. "I guess my son here will stick with water."

Conrad nodded that water was fine and the waitress went off to the bar. He looked at his father. This man had taught him to shoot and hunt, fly fish and ride. He'd talked to him frankly about women from the time Conrad was eight years old and August had caught him looking through an old *Playboy*. August had outlined the best strategies when in pursuit of tail, graphic details about technique and approach. It had at first upset Conrad to learn that his father wasn't faithful to his mother but, with time, he came to accept his father's belief that no one woman was enough for a real man. Normal rules simply didn't apply to Wentworths; a lesson Conrad learned early and well. His father showed him the ins and outs of privilege and the lessons had kept them close all the way through high school. August had been the king of the world then, bigger than life, Conrad's hero.

The waitress brought the drinks and August winked at her again. She didn't seem to notice his rather pathetic attempt at flirtation and walked quickly away from the table. August cleared his throat then took a long pull on his drink.

"Your mother wanted me to ask you about those damn tongs."

"Yeah, she called me."

"You didn't find them?"

Conrad shook his head. "I'm sure they'll turn up."

"They'd better." August took the toothpick out of his glass and ate the olives. "Otherwise we're going to have to fly back to Vienna and find her another tea set. Pain in the butt."

Going East to college had changed everything for Conrad. He was surrounded by arrogant, hard working kids, just like himself, who expected nothing less than surrender from the world in which they lived. California was considered a joke and Conrad had to work very hard to prove himself worthy of their friendship. Many of these students came from old families with connections to wealth and power that made August seem absurdly provincial.

These were educated people, unlike his father who may or may not have finished college, and the more time Conrad spent with them, the smaller his father became until one morning Conrad woke up and realized that August was nothing but an overly pampered clown, and not a particularly bright one at that. It was a liberating realization and it set Conrad free. From that moment forward, he rebuilt his self-image according to his own rules and discarded August as a role model.

August blew out a great gust of air and settled into his seat. If you looked closely you could see the broken blood vessels on his nose and blotchiness in his cheeks. It was amazing that this man could drink as much as he did and still look so healthy, so vibrant. But Conrad suspected it was an illusion. The guy must be rotting from the inside out, only a matter of time.

"The thing is, she's twenty-one and she loves me." August took another sip of the martini, his second. "Tell me you could resist twenty-one."

"So Angela thinks you're helping the kid." Conrad cut into his steak and took a bite. His father hadn't touched his food yet. "Big deal."

"No. She knows." August speared another olive and popped it in his mouth. "Just like your mother. You know how she looks at you when she knows? Exactly like that." He drained his glass and held it up, expectantly.

"And you're worried that what?" Conrad looked at his father. His mouth was starting to sag with the alcohol. "She's going to tell on you? Come on, Dad."

August shook his head, picked up his knife and fork, and started in on the bloody steak. "She's trouble." He chewed with his mouth open. "Trouble with a capital T."

"So you're warning me." This was taking far too long and his father was definitely getting drunk. "Because Angela's not an issue."

"There are certain kinds of women, Conrad. Dangerous ones."

August put his knife and fork down on the plate. "I know you've been out there but this broad... She's ruthless, all teeth and claws. She wants something from us."

"You're talking 95 percent of the female population." Conrad drank his water. "98 percent. I can handle it."

"I don't know." August's third martini arrived. "It worries me."

"Everything's okay." Conrad reached over and patted his father's hand. "I'll take care of it."

"You ever get dizzy? Suddenly, out of the blue, you're all disoriented? Like you don't know where you are?" August looked into Conrad's eyes. "That ever happen to you?"

"Come on." Conrad laughed and gently took the drink from his father's hand. He set it on the corner of the table, just out of reach. "Eat some food."

"I'm just saying, be careful." August cut into his steak. "We all need to be real careful."

37

Ask Miss Katie

*D*ear Miss Katie:

For the last week or so I've been waking up in the morning not knowing where I am. I look around my bedroom and don't recognize my own belongings. I don't know who I am or why I'm here. I've lived in this house and been married to this same woman for seventeen years but somehow, in the mornings, everything looks strange and slightly hostile to me. I feel scared and hopeless for the first couple minutes of consciousness then I start to remember my life and the fear subsides. But still, I don't always want to get out of bed. I'm wondering, is this normal for a forty-two-year-old man?

My wife and I are happily married and have two kids, thirteen and fifteen. I think my son may have a little problem with stealing and I discovered drug paraphernalia in my daughter's room but both kids are good students, so I'm hoping that these problems are just typical teenage issues that will work themselves out. My wife tends to get overly excited about the smallest little thing, she's a nervous type of person who sometimes needs medication, so I don't really want to burden her with the kids' problems especially since I think they're not such a big deal. But I'm not that comfortable with keeping secrets and I wonder if that could be contributing to my morning confusion.

I had a surgical procedure to correct a snoring problem that my wife found intolerable, and now I suffer from dry mouth. But otherwise I am in excellent health. Do other people wake up foggy or do you think I have a real problem?

Signed,
Muddled

38

Miss Katie Says

Dear Muddled,

Your solution could be as simple as a new mattress, a good air purifier and a fresh set of sheets, but I don't think so. Kleptomaniac son, drug-using daughter, overly medicated wife and you don't want to get out of bed in the mornings. HELLO. Not normal, I don't care how old you are. These are real problems and you have to DO SOMETHING right away. You need to stop tiptoeing around the issues and talk to your wife. Your wife needs to lay off the pills and pick up the parental reins. You and she need to start working as a team because your kids are in trouble. Do you want your boy to end up in jail? Do you want your daughter to drop out of school? That's the road you're on. I say run, don't walk, to the nearest professional. Get your son in therapy, your daughter in rehab, and gather round in one big circle for a few good hours of family counseling. It is your job as a parent to sort out this mess. Get busy!

Miss Katie

P.S. Let me know how it all turns out. I really care.

39

Group Dynamics

The Wentworth-Jones family sat around a coffee table in the therapist's office. Joey held the smooth river rock in his lap and Dr. Rosenblatt wanted to know how he felt about his father.

Joey turned to Paul. "Fucking pirate."

"Pirate," Dr. Rosenblatt said. "That's very good Joey."

"It's my room." Joey savagely tore a piece of flesh off his thumb. "You had no right to sneak in there and take my stuff."

Monica snorted and said, "Your stuff..."

"Monica." Dr. Rosenblatt held up his hand to stop her. "Joey has the talking piece. When he's finished I'll have him pass the rock to you but for now we must respect his turn and listen."

Monica rolled her eyes.

"Go on, Joey." Dr. Rosenblatt held his pen over his note pad, ready to scribble down any relevant tidbits as they came spilling out.

"Everyone can just fuck off." Joey switched from thumb to index finger. "This is stupid."

"Pirates, Joey," Dr. Rosenblatt said. "Can you talk about pirates? What do pirates do? They steal. They invade. They plunder. Do you feel violated by what your father did?"

"I'll give the stuff back, okay?" Joey said. "I won't take any-more junk if we just end this? I'll call grandma and tell her I took the tongs . . ."

"You will do no such thing." Becky stood up. Her voice was loud and threatening. "Mother will never find out. Clear? No one will ever find out. This is private."

"Rebecca." Dr. Rosenblatt stood and took her arm. "You can not interrupt the person who holds the stone. We've been over this. I don't want to make you leave the circle but I will if you don't control your outbursts."

"Excuse me." Becky pulled her arm away. "I'm paying you, right?"

"Everyone follows the rules or there's no point." Dr. Rosenblatt tried to ease Becky back into her seat but she resisted.

"You don't understand the dynamics of my family, Doctor." Becky slashed the air with her index finger. "There's a lot at stake and I can't afford to have my children labeled as troublemakers. My mother could turn on us and then where would we be? There's college and trust funds . . ."

Dr. Rosenblatt caught her hand and lowered it forcefully to her side as he said, "When Joey's finished . . ."

"I'm finished." Joey tossed the stone onto the coffee table where it landed with a loud crack. Dr. Rosenblatt dropped his note pad, fell to his knees and ran his fingers over the surface of the table. There was a scratch where the rock had landed but the glass did not break. He wet his index finger and worked the mark, try-ing to erase the damage. Monica snatched up the stone.

"I'd like to know what the good doctor thinks about the fact that my mother is obsessed with my weight and my sex life."

"That is a goddamn lie." Becky's nostrils flared. "How dare you accuse me? I don't even know how much you weigh. And as far as sex... You're not having sex, are you? Are you having sex? Oh my God, Paul."

Dr. Rosenblatt stood up and sighed, whether because of his scratched table or Becky's outburst was unclear. "Rebecca, I'm going to have to ask you to please sit in the corner chair. You can rejoin the circle when you've calmed yourself."

Rebecca didn't move. Paul stood and hugged her. He whispered in her ear, "I know it's hard, but this is for the family." Becky hesitated. "Please, sweetheart."

Becky walked over and threw herself in the chair.

"Please continue, Monica," Dr. Rosenblatt said. "You were saying how you feel that your mother has an inappropriate interest in your personal life and your physicality."

"Is it weird that she examines my underpants all the time, Doctor? Cause that's what she does. I've seen her standing by the washing machine. She examines them and accuses me of stuff."

"Fifteen is too young to be having sex." Becky jumped up out of the chair. "It's that Cushner boy, the one who drives you to school, isn't it?"

Monica ignored her mother. "I am not having sex. But if I was, wouldn't that be my business, Dr. Rosenblatt?"

"Her underpants are often stiff," Becky said. "And why would a fifteen year old want thong underwear if she wasn't having sex?"

"That is disgusting." Joey put his hands over his ears. "I don't want to hear about my sister's underpants."

Paul flinched and turned a dark red.

Dr. Rosenblatt frowned and made some notes.

"I've seen how she acts around that boy." Rebecca was talking fast now. She knew that at any moment she'd be cut off. "She gets all breathless and giggly. That's not the way to get a boy, Monica. Acting all stupid isn't going to impress him. He's just using you, you know..."

Dr. Rosenblatt stood up and grabbed Rebecca forcefully by the arm. She immediately surrendered and he guided her out of the room. Monica looked at Paul and said, "I'm not having sex. I don't even like him."

Paul sat very still. This was uncharted territory. He held his breath, waiting for Dr. Rosenblatt to reenter and show them how to proceed.

Dr. Rosenblatt came back into the room. "We've made some progress here today." He smiled. "Opened up some new doors, I think. Your assignment for next time is to write down five things you admire about each family member, including yourself, and five things you'd like to see change. We'll review the lists and discuss them. Remember, we are trying to be CONSTRUCTIVE, not DESTRUCTIVE."

"What about my mother?" Monica said.

"Your mother has promised to follow the rules. No confrontations outside of this office. Make notes. Understand?"

Paul, Monica and Joey nodded.

"Good work. See you on Wednesday."

40

Norman Wants to Play

When Norman heard the Wentworth-Jones family was seeing a psychologist, a light bulb switched on. Therapy. Even the word itself was soothing. He wanted in. Norman had problems too, why shouldn't he get help? Three, four, five times a week, someone listening to him, focusing on him, exclusively discussing his dilemmas and pressing issues. The idea was enormously appealing. He wondered, would the good doctor seat him in a chair or on a couch? Would he lie down? Would there be a clean paper mat on the pillow to keep everything fresh, or would that pillow be soaked through with other people's hair secretions, stale and smelly? He would have to bring his own protection, just in case. Nothing worse than the stench of dirty hair.

Norman wasn't going to be one of those patients who spent the whole hour complaining about his mother. No simple Oedipal issues in his head, no penis envy either. Oh no, Norman had far bigger issues. The therapist would be impressed by how deep Norman's problems actually ran. Jung, Freud, Kubler-Ross, Dr. Zachary Smith—it was all very exciting.

Of course he was going to go to Becky's doctor. No question about that. The man was a family therapist and Norman was part of the family. Maybe Norman could be helpful to his sister's progress by shedding some light on her early years, revealing to the good doctor some of those forgotten moments in her past, things Becky might not have gotten around to mentioning. It just made sense.

Becky thought the whole thing was a secret. She would be devastated if she knew the cat was out of the bag. But if she wanted to keep things private, she should consider putting a muzzle on Paul or, better yet, have his vocal cords severed. Paul spilled the beans to August in one of his "getting close" phone calls and Norman was right there eavesdropping on the extension, fulfilling his duty as family archivist. August merely grunted at the news but Norman felt the big bubbles of euphoria floating up through his consciousness. Things were not so perfect in Becky's little world? How sad. He jotted the name down, Dr. Rosenblatt, and waited patiently while Paul droned on about Becky's allergies and his deep longing for a puppy. Finally the call ended and Norman was able to make his first appointment.

41

*Highlights of the Wentworth-Jones'
Personality Lists*

PAUL ON PAUL

PROS	CONS
1. Paul is a good listener	1. Paul is often indecisive
2. Paul is patient	2. Paul isn't sensitive enough
3. Paul is loyal	3. Paul needs to watch his diet
4. Paul cares	4. Paul cracks his knuckles
5. Paul can change	5. Paul still snores

MONICA ON BECKY

She's a good skier—She's a total bitch

She has good taste in shoes—She never listens

She says what she thinks—She yells at everyone

She's got nice hair—She's way too vain

She remembers people's names—She's never hugged me

BECKY ON PAUL

GOOD

1. Paul is a good father. He has always been willing to do math homework with the kids and proofread their English papers.

2. Paul is very conscientious about household chores. He takes out the trash on the weekends when Lucy's not there and usually does the dishes.

3. Paul never forgets a birthday and he's pretty good about gifts.

4. Paul would never have an affair.

5. Paul doesn't get in bad moods.

BAD

1. Paul is often dense. I don't know if it's because he's hard of hearing, or he just doesn't pay attention, or maybe it's just a man thing, but often I have to repeat and explain the stupidest things. For example: I don't do dairy. The whole mucous thing plus it really irritates my IBS. I've told him this like a hundred thousand times, right? It's basically a medical situation so you'd think he'd remember. But no. He still brings me lattes with nonfat milk when the only thing I can tolerate is soy. How hard is that? And grains. I've given up all grains for the same reason—which is really, really hard, by the way—but Paul still passes me the breadbasket when we go to restaurants. I mean, why would he torture me with that kind of temptation? Why not just put the bread on the other side of the table where I don't have to see it? That kind of stuff.

2. Paul's way of showing affection is to scratch me behind the ears. Not really scratch, more like rub, but I'm not a dog. Does that sound like a turn on, to be treated like a Schnauzer? I remind him, over and over, and he apologizes but then when we're watching TV or driving in the car, out comes the hand. It makes me nuts.

3. Whenever we have an argument, Paul apologizes. Now I have to admit that sometimes I might not be the easiest person to live with. I've got hormonal issues and stuff, so I'm not always right. I mean sometimes in the

middle of a fight I even know that the point I'm arguing is wrong, not fair. But Paul always backs down. He always accepts the blame even when it's not his fault. That's not right. He should stand up for himself. It's hard to respect a man who doesn't act like a man.

4. Paul clears his throat constantly. I took him to a doctor, after he had his surgery, and the doctor said there's no reason for him to be doing it. Basically it's just a habit. He doesn't have to make that noise, there's nothing lodged, no cancer. I think he does it for attention. It's his way of announcing his presence in a room, get people to notice him. Well, it drives everyone crazy and it's another stellar example of his insensitivity.

5. Paul spends way too much time around the house. I mean, it's good for a husband and father to be concerned about his family but we're his entire universe and sometimes it's a bit much. Why can't he take up golf or something? Get out with some buddies. Instead he wants to go with me to my yoga class. Come on, yoga with Paul? I don't think so.

Part Two

1

Jack Belmont
(Honey's Ex)

A Pretty Decent Guy From
a Different Kind of Family

My mother died. I hadn't seen or thought about her for years and then I got this telegram. I don't know how they found me, I guess they can find anybody if it's important enough. Pretty much all it said was that she died and that I needed to come back and deal with it. Weird. When I close my eyes I can't even come up with a vague sketch of what she looked like. It's been that long. She was a quiet type, my mother. Medium everything, I think. Maybe brown hair? Yeah, brown. She had brown eyes too, I remember that 'cause mine were so blue and I always figured that my father must have had super-strong genes to overcome that brown thing. Seems like Mother should have been able to identify him as my father—the guy with the really blue eyes. But according to her, there was no way to know for sure. She couldn't pick him out of a lineup and so the crime of my inception went unsolved. I don't think she really tried to find him. She just wanted to pretend the whole thing never happened, only I was there to remind her of it every day. Mother was not a happy woman, that much I do remember.

I'm driving back, heading down the 99, destination Exeter,

which is next to Farmersville and Lindsay and Lemon Cove and Visalia. It's in the general vicinity of Fresno and a million other shit-hole farm towns. Same, same, same, one town to the next. Actually, the look of the place has changed since I was last here. Arby's, Wendy's, Appleby's, Del Taco, Taco Bell, Jack-in-the-Box, Burger King, McDonald's, Carl's Junior, KFC: apparently these are the primary food sources for our great nation today. Gone are most of the crops and citrus trees along this stretch of the 99. Asphalt, concrete and stucco appear to be the fertilizers of the tweny-first century. Pour a foundation, up sprouts a strip mall. Level the orange groves and bring in rows and rows of track housing. Every now and then there are still open spaces, fields where produce struggles up out of the ground with the gentle dusting of auto exhaust, diesel fumes and a healthy dose of pesticides but mostly what I'm looking at is urban sprawl and smog. Don't get me wrong, I'm definitely not waxing nostalgic for a time gone by. In my opinion, this valley was, and is, the armpit of our Golden State. Hot dusty summers, gray damp winters and a whole lot of nothing to do. Small minds with big problems. Petty crime was the sport I played in high school, breaking and entering my specialty. My mother, and the whole town of Exeter, were ready to see me go by the time I graduated.

My mother's name was Claire. Claire Belmont. She was nineteen when I was born. I can't tell you much more about her life. I guess I was never very interested. I don't think she was even interested in her life. There was the rape story, but now, come to think of it, who knows if that was true. She might have had a boyfriend or a lover. There could have been a scandal. It's impossible to say what kind of person Claire Belmont was before I came along. She might have been a young, lovely girl on the edge of an exciting life when fate pulled the rug out from under her. She may have had hopes and dreams. Who knows? All I can tell you is that the woman I grew up with was almost invisible there in the house with my grandparents. I don't remember her laughter or her tears. What I come up with are three disappointed adults shuffling around, from room to room, in a house where the curtains were always drawn and voices kept to a low murmur. Shame and guilt and sadness. Then, when I was around eight or nine, the grandparents expired and it was just Claire and me in that big dark house. You think she might have come to life then, with the parents gone. She could have started again, had a life. But no, nothing changed. Our house was filled with one silent mother and one unhappy boy dreaming of escape.

Seems like, when someone dies, there should be an organization or something that comes to straighten things up, a government agency that rushes over to the house to tie up loose ends and comfort anyone left behind, an official condolence committee. Shouldn't there be efficient procedures and understanding agents? And shouldn't there be someone in charge who cares or at least pretends to care like those priests who perform funerals for people they never met? At least those preachers pretend to mourn the 0 you're just gone and nobody's gonna miss you. You're reduced to a series of forms and all that's left of you is a little bit of paperwork. The world's not even gonna skip a beat and that does not seem right to me. My mother died and nobody cares and that's just wrong.

2

Norman on the Perfect Man

I've always felt a deep connection with the Marlboro Man. He was perfect, sitting there on his horse in that suede vest and worn shirt, cowboy hat, squinting into the sun, scanning the horizon. His lips and that cigarette, how could you not smoke? I studied how he sat in the saddle, reins in hand, boots secured in the stirrups. I wanted to be his horse. Can you imagine? The Marlboro Man riding me. Giddy-up. I would have taken him out at a full gallop; you know I would. The Marlboro Man haunted my dreams, still does. The model changed over the years but my attraction never wavered. My perfect man is a smoker.

He must have nice nail beds. I can't tolerate stubby hands. Long fingers, in my experience, indicate a superior level of sensitivity. Swollen knuckles—deal breaker. I won't even consider a man who's spent his life cracking.

Yes on full lips, but the mouth has to be masculine. Some of the models today with those girly mouths? Not my thing. I'm not into boyish either. I want a full-grown man, preferably with a scruffy beard. Understand that once I get him back to my place, I'll have to shave his face—whisker burn. But for that initial attraction? Let the beard grow.

My perfect man drives a truck. Probably never washes it. Or maybe he does because if you don't wash your car it rusts. Right? I'm not sure about that. If you need to wash your car in order to take care of it, then he would wash his truck from time to time because he is not a wasteful person.

My man is very handy. He can fix anything. The mysteries of plumbing and electrical are simple problems for him. He can take apart your engine and put it back together with his eyes closed. Your horse is going lame? He can ascertain the problem and provide a cure for your beloved animal. Build a house? Sail a boat? No problem.

Money means nothing to the perfect man. He is about experience and adventure. His values wouldn't even register on the L.A. Richter scale. There's a purity to his spirit unheard of in this city.

He's tough. He's been through it and the lines on his face are a map of hard lessons. He's been hurt, spent a lot of lonely nights, and he's broken many hearts, but underneath it all, he's decent. He will always do the right thing in the long run.

What I can tell you, with absolute certainty, is they don't grow them like that here. You will not find a perfect man in Los Angeles. Or if you do, he's just passing through. This town would not hold his interest. He would not be fooled by the thin veneer of this ersatz culture. No. He is a product of a different place and perhaps a different time. And when he loves, he will love deeply and forever.

3

Welcome Home, Jack

The house looked the same. Faded blue stucco box set on a
dusty patch of barren ground. The curtains were drawn in those
small windows, the fabric yellowed by the years of relentless sun.
Jack parked the truck on the street and walked the fifteen feet to
the door. The octagonal concrete paving stones were still set in
dirt and he made a point of stepping on each one just as he had as
a boy even though they were set too close together for an adult
stride. Jack remembered how muddy this yard got during the rains
and how he would perch on that last stone making mud pies until
his mother would catch him and force him to go inside where she
would scrub his hands with a soapy nail brush and insist that he
stop causing trouble. Jack could hear her telling him to hush.
Always be quiet. Don't make a sound.

There was one sad tree off to the left of the house. This was a
tree whose frail trunk barely supported the canopy of brittle leaves.
The too few branches never filled in enough for climbing nor did
they offer much shade during those blistering hot summers. It was
a useless tree to a lonely boy and as far as Jack could tell it hadn't
changed or grown a single inch in all the years since he left. Jack
walked over and ran his hand along the scarred backside of the

trunk. The deep slashes that he'd made as a child were still there, dark now like a cattle brand, but clear. They were the marks of an angry boy and he could remember how good it felt to cut that tree and dig at it with his sharp knife.

So here he was, at the house where he grew up, his family's house, searching for something familiar, a feeling that he belonged, a hint of comfort. But Jack didn't feel anything. This house could be anywhere and belong to anyone. It was as anonymous as the other twenty identical stucco boxes that lined this sorry block. Whatever history he had with this place was meaningless to him now. Standing there on that front step, Jack felt for the first time that he was alone. He'd spent his life moving from one town to the next, never settling long enough to form any real connections, and now he was as invisible to the world as his dead mother. He could shoot himself in the head, right here, right this minute, and no one would care.

Jack put the house key back into the envelope and walked to his car. There wasn't anything in that house for him. He didn't need to go inside. He would return the packet to the lawyer and sign the papers. They could sell everything, send him a check. Jack Belmont needed to get out of Exeter, right now. Jack Belmont needed to get a life.

4

Heart to Heart with Conrad

"*I* didn't take your mother's fucking tongs."

"You're like every other bottom feeder out there with a pussy and a pair of legs."

"I swear I didn't. I don't even remember seeing them."

"Do you know who I am, Angela?"

"I'll call her and tell her myself."

"What I'm capable of?"

"Give me her number."

"You are not calling anyone. Stay the fuck away."

"You know Conrad, another few weeks and the baby will start kicking. Pretty exciting."

"That's not going to work, stupid bitch."

"I just think your family would want to be a part of this. A new grandchild? It's not fair to exclude them."

"Listen, 'cause I'm only going to say this once: Disappear. One way or the other—up to you. I don't want to hear another word about Angela Simms from anyone. Got it? I'm going out of town and when I get back, you're gone. You never existed."

5

If Wishes Were Fishes

What Honey didn't expect was for Miss Angela to turn all friendly. Honey had been fairly certain that Gus could pull some strings and get Kimmy back into the Happy Helpers. She assumed that he threw money at the problem and made it go away. Was there anything that money couldn't fix? But Honey never imagined, not in her wildest dreams, that snobby Miss Angela would change her tune.

First there was the phone call:

"Honey," Miss Angela said. "I've made a terrible mistake and I need you to forgive me."

Honey didn't even have a clue how to respond to Miss Angela begging so she stayed quiet on the other end of the phone.

"We need Kimmy here, with us, where she belongs. It's all my fault." Miss Angela cleared her throat and lowered her voice. "Honey, I've been having a lot of trouble with mood swings. Do you ever have mood swings?"

"Not really," said Honey.

"Well, bad moods. You have those sometimes, don't you?"

"Sure."

"Sometimes I feel like the blood in my body turns poison and I just lash out. Hurt those that I care about the most. Do you ever feel like that, Honey? Like some sort of viper?"

"I don't know."

"I did it to you. You and little Kimmy. Two of the sweetest people at Happy Helpers." Miss Angela's voice caught. She was definitely choking back tears. "I switched medications about a week ago. I think I had a bad reaction, obviously I did, and you were the victim."

"Wow," Honey said. She couldn't believe it but she actually felt bad. "What kind of medicine?"

"Antidepressants." Miss Angela blew her nose and it was loud. Honey held the phone a few inches from her ear until Miss Angela finished. "I just can't tolerate Prozac and the Welbutrin doesn't seem to work at all. Personal problems. It's a mess. But the point is, I'm sorry and I really want you back at the school. Will you come back? Please? I promise I will make everything right."

"Okay," Honey said. "Sure."

"Thank God," Angela said. "Everybody was so mad at me when I threw my psychotic little fit. The staff and the children just love Kimmy. She's very popular. They'll be so relieved."

Honey knew that Angela was making that last part up. Kimmy was a great kid, but she was not one of the favorites at Happy Helpers. Angela was obviously the kind of person who just had to exaggerate everything. Lots of people were like that. So Honey accepted the invitation to reenroll and marched Kimmy back to preschool the very next morning, much to Kimmy's dismay.

A few days after the phone call, Angela invited Honey for coffee. They walked around the corner from the school to the local Starbucks. Angela was so nice, she'd obviously found the right medicine, and the two of them sat there for over an hour just yapping away. Actually it was Honey who did most of the talking. Once she started, she just couldn't stop and before she knew it, she'd told Angela the whole story about her father dying and Colorado City and Kimmy and Jack and the heartbreak she suffered when he left her. It felt so good to talk. Honey heard herself say, out loud for the first time, "I'm still in love with Jack Belmont. I guess I'll always be in love with him." And Angela took her hand and squeezed it tight. They were becoming friends, real friends, and Honey felt she could talk about anything. Anything but Gus. He was a secret she did not want to share. If Angela asked, Honey would say he was like a father to her or a grandfather, but Angela didn't ask.

And now there was an invitation to dinner, just the two girls. A real night on the town, Honey's first. Her neighbor, Mrs. Rappaport, volunteered to baby-sit and Kimmy was happy to go, so now all Honey had to worry about was what to wear. What to wear? Miss Angela, *Angela*, was always so stylish with her beautiful shoes and slim-fitting pants and skirts. Even on the days when she actually worked with the children she looked like a model in her casual clothes. Honey opened the closet. Her wardrobe consisted of dull, graying synthetics. No-iron cotton/poly blouses, stretch pants, old-fashioned jeans. Honey pulled out the jeans and held them up. High-waisted pants went out long before Kimmy was born. Honey had never felt so stupid or so ugly in her entire life. She didn't have any nice clothes and even if she did, she'd still be a geek.

Maybe she shouldn't go. She could call Angela and say she was sick or Kimmy was sick. But Angela would probably just reschedule and then Honey would have to go through this all over again. Or maybe Angela wouldn't reschedule and that would be even worse. So Honey took a deep breath and sorted through every article of clothing in that sorry closet and the best she could come up with was a black stretchy skirt that she wore to work sometimes and a purple fuzzy sweater. It wasn't fancy, but it wasn't too embarrassing either. She put on some mascara and lip-gloss, brushed her hair and teeth, and promised herself that she would not look in the mirror again for the rest of the evening. This was about friendship and Honey was not going to let her unhip-ugliness ruin the night.

Angela was late. It was difficult, waiting, and Honey was tempted to go take one hard last look at her horribleness or maybe even cancel but she resisted. God was presenting her with a friend and she was not going to pass up his offer. It was funny but this was the first time God had entered her thoughts since she left Colorado City. God, who had been responsible for so many things in her life. Her father's death. Her stepfather and those horrible church elders. Jack Belmont's delivery trunk. Kimmy and all the hard times since.

But He worked in mysterious ways and even though His benevolence seemed to have been absent from her life for so many years, it looked like He was smiling on her again. The tide was finally changing and with that positive thought in mind, Honey sat on the edge of the chair by the front door and waited for Angela.

The bell rang at twenty past seven. Finally. Honey sprang up and opened the door. Angela wore jeans, a white tank top, a black leather jacket and biker boots. She looked great but very casual.

"Oh," Honey said. "I think I'm wearing the wrong thing. Should I change real quick?"

"Noooo." Angela gave her a hug and walked into the apartment. "You look great."

Honey had been hoping that Angela wouldn't come in. The apartment was a dump and she was embarrassed by the dumb furniture and Kimmy's finger paintings that were taped up on the walls. But really, friends hung out at each other's places. Friends didn't judge each other and it wasn't a bad apartment, just dingy and plain.

"Great apartment." Angela flopped down on the couch.

"Do you want something?" Honey motioned towards the kitchen. "Tequila?"

Honey could feel her face heat up. She didn't have tequila, she didn't have any alcohol in the house, not even beer. Those were things that adults had and Honey wasn't living in that world. She spent her days in a mindless job serving coffee and never really talking to anyone. Gus came and went but he wasn't interested in Honey's feelings or thoughts. Did she even have thoughts beyond basic survival? Her only friend was Kimmy and they spent most of their time watching TV. Honey was in over her head. All she could offer was juice, soda and 2% milk and suddenly she felt like this whole evening was a very stupid idea. She looked at Angela and shook her head sadly. Maybe Angela would take pity on her and just leave.

"Well then, we're just going to have to go find some." Angela stood and headed for the door.

This was the moment that Honey could have ended it. She could have said that she suddenly didn't feel well. That the babysitter fell through. That the truth was there wasn't any point in going out, because eventually Angela would realize how stupid and boring she was and then she'd dump her and why not just save time and call the whole thing off. If Honey just told the truth, she could get Angela out of there in two minutes. She could say that she'd changed her mind and that she didn't think it was a good idea to socialize with the head of Kimmy's school. She could get a migraine. But Honey didn't have the strength to resist and so she grabbed her purse and followed Angela out of the apartment.

"If a guy runs his tongue down my back and kisses the base of my spine, I'm history." Angela picked up the shot glass of tequila and threw it back. "I actually love to have my ass kissed too."

"Yeah," Honey laughed. They'd been sitting in this bar all night and things were starting to get fuzzy but she was pretty sure that Angela had just made a joke. Honey drank her shot of tequila and said, "Who doesn't like to have their ass kissed?"

Angela looked into her eyes. "What else do you like, Honey?"

"I don't know." Honey hadn't minded the talk about sex as long as she could just be a spectator but she couldn't possibly say anything about herself.

Angela signaled the waiter for more drinks then said, "Do you like to have your breasts kissed?"

Honey crossed her arms over her chest and looked at the table. She was embarrassed but she also felt the damp heat between her legs. She liked it and so she forced herself to meet Angela's eyes. "Yeah, I like that."

"Licking the sides and underneath? Round and round your nipples with the tongue."

"Yeah."

"Are your nipples sensitive?"

"Uh huh."

"Mine too." Angela brushed her hand across her perfect right breast. She wasn't wearing a bra and Honey could see her stiffen. "I like to have my nipples sucked and then pulled with the teeth, gently. I can almost come just from that."

Honey could see that now both of Angela's nipples were erect. She had perfect tits, small and high. Her shirt was so transparent it was impossible not to look.

"And I liked to be teased. I don't want to get down to business too fast. So many people are goal oriented when it comes to sex. You know?"

Honey nodded. She had no idea what Angela was talking about.

"They jump into bed and all they want to do is have the big orgasm. A few acrobatics and kaboom. Not me. I mean I'm going to have my orgasm, probably a bunch of them, but I want to go all night. I want to be on the brink a hundred times before I give in. I want it to be about my whole body, not just the parts, ya know? The rhythm, up and down, in and out. And I want to kiss and suck and fuck until . . ."

The waiter arrived with the tequila. He was tall and blond, very good looking, and he definitely heard what Angela had just said. He smiled at her, sex written all over his face. He set the drinks down and said, "Can I do anything else for you ladies?"

"Not a thing." Angela was annoyed at the interruption, her voice cold and dismissive. The waiter hesitated and stared at Angela's clearly visible nipples. He wanted her to acknowledge him, but she would not look up. Honey would have smiled if he'd looked her way. He was gorgeous and the alcohol and sex talk made her feel wild and open in a way she'd hadn't since before Kimmy was born. It was how Jack use to make her feel. Hungry and insatiable. Yeah, she would have smiled at that cute waiter. She probably would have gone off to the alley or back room with him if he'd just asked. But he didn't. He stood beside Angela waiting for her attention. Finally she said, "The check. You can bring us the check."

There had been more tequila back at Angela's house. That much, Honey knew. Tequila and maybe bourbon? Scotch? Something brown. Honey was lying in her bed. It was dark but it felt too hard to roll over and check the clock. Her head hurt and her body felt so sick, so filled with poison, that all she could do was lie still. She had no memory of coming home, in fact, the last part of the evening was completely blank.

Honey sat up suddenly, shot through with panic. Where was Kimmy? There was nothing about Kimmy in her memory bank. She got up out of bed, still in her black skirt and purple sweater, and rushed into Kimmy's room. Her daughter was sleeping soundly, tucked in under her pink quilt. Somehow she'd gotten home. Probably Honey had gone to get her at Mrs. Rappaport's apartment. Undoubtedly there'd been some kind of conversation, some slurry babbling thank you. What had she done? What kind of mother has blackouts?

Honey walked back to her bedroom and stripped off her clothes. She lay down on the bed and forced herself to reconstruct as much of the evening as she could.

They'd driven from the restaurant back to Angela's house. Honey remembered waving to the waiter on the way out and giggling in the car with Angela about his cute butt. The drinking. They'd talked. Honey talked about Jack, Angela hugged her. Honey cried. Oh God. The Jacuzzi. Somehow they ended up in the Jacuzzi. Naked. Honey curled into a ball. The very idea that Angela had seen her body without clothes. Shit. And Honey could remember Angela's body, all sleek and tanned with those pretty breasts. Did they touch? Honey wanted to last night, she knew that. And the dread that maybe she'd made some kind of inappropriate move. But wouldn't Honey remember if she had? Honey sat up. She did remember, she didn't want to, but there it was. She had kissed Angela. She'd leaned over and kissed her and run her fingers across her collarbone and down between her breasts. And Angela's lips were so soft, not like a man's at all. It felt so right. Angela kissed her back. And they touched each other and Angela asked if Honey had been with anyone since Jack and Honey told her about Gus. She told her everything while Angela stroked her nipples and kissed her neck.

Did this mean that Honey was a lesbian? She fell back into the pillows. She'd been with a woman, wanted to be with a woman, but now it seemed so ugly and wrong. It was disgusting. What happened next? They obviously got out of the Jacuzzi at some point but that was lost. The rest of the evening was gone.

6

Norman on the Couch

*N*orman lay on the couch gazing at the poorly framed Chagall. He hated Chagall, all those flying people with cows and goats. It was a poster, not a print, probably purchased on the Venice boardwalk: two for the price of one. Everything in the room was cheap: the acrylic rug, the no-stain upholstery.

"Norman?" Dr. Rosenblatt said. "I asked you how you felt when Little Mister Swissick got lost. You said you thought your mother might have thrown him away?"

"I don't remember."

"Sit up." Dr. Rosenblatt cleared his throat. "Norman, I want you to sit up. We're going to try a different approach."

Norman sat up. What he wanted to do was go to sleep but Dr. Rosenblatt would never allow him even a second's peace. The constant prodding and poking of his tender mind was becoming extremely aggravating. He found himself anxious most of the time and often worried about a brain hemorrhage. Why did he ever open this can of worms?

"There are many types of therapy and theories about analysis." Dr. Rosenblatt got up from his chair and joined Norman on the couch. "Cognitive, Attachment, Reality Therapy, Choice Therapy,

Phenomenology, Womb Envy, Primal Explorations. I've studied all these and more. There is no single answer, Norman. Different things work for different people. It all boils down to pain."

Why did Norman feel like a puppy that'd wet on the carpet and was now being punished with a rolled-up newspaper? Why did Norman want to cry?

"We're trying to get past your *survival mind* and your *thinking mind* to your *feeling mind*," Dr. Rosenblatt said. "I'm going to hold your hand. No one's ever really done that for you, have they?"

Norman yawned. He was completely exhausted.

"Together we are going to break down your defenses because they are simply agents of repression," Dr. Rosenblatt took Norman's hand. "You don't need them anymore. Your defenses consume energy while protecting your system from the cata-strophic PAIN of unfulfilled need."

Norman tried to pull away, Dr. Rosenblatt's hand was sticky, but Dr. Rosenblatt squeezed hard and wouldn't let go.

"Once we recognize the pain, it simply becomes a feeling." Dr. Rosenblatt scooted over and pulled Norman into a fatherly hug. "I'm here for you. We're going to do this together."

Dr. Rosenblatt released Norman from the hug, held his hand again, then settled back into the couch. "Make yourself comfort-able, Norman. We're about to embark on a fascinating journey."

Norman leaned back into the cushions. What choice did he have? The two men sat there together, holding hands, staring out at the drab and poorly-appointed office of Dr. Harold Rosenblatt, like an old married couple waiting for the evening news.

7

While Honey's Hungover, Angela's Making Headway

Angela finished her cup of coffee as she watched Judith Wentworth pull into the parking lot and wait in the long line of cars. Angela left some money on the table then ran across the street and ducked down behind the bright yellow Hummer just as Judith pulled up to the valet station.

"Good morning, Mrs. Wentworth," the Hispanic parking attendant said. He was a short man with a pronounced limp and a withered hand.

"Pedro." Judith accepted the ticket. "All's well?"

"Perfect, Mrs. Wentworth." Pedro hobbled to the car and hoisted his sad body up into the seat. "Everything is perfect."

Judith walked to the entrance of Salon Faberge and went inside for her biweekly hair appointment with Graziano. Angela smiled. Honey had been such a big help; she'd known virtually every detail about the Wentworth household.

Faberge, the mecca of beauty in Beverly Hills, was a virtual beehive of activity. Busy hairdressers faced life altering decisions. Assistants fetched decaf nonfat cappuccinos or triple espressos for the valued clients. Apprentices washed hair or folded pieces of foil for the delicate and artful highlights that the master colorists strove to create. Brow and eyelash tinting, facial waxing in the front room, Brazilians in the back. All the employees dressed in black, all the clients wrapped in purple gowns and white, white towels. Very uniform and chic. Snipping and cutting and endless sweeping of the floor all accompanied by a subtle but insistent beat of the hip, yet soothing, (and vaguely suggestive) background music.

Angela watched as Judith was greeted like royalty with a kiss and deeply felt hug by the twenty-year-old receptionist then led to one of the stations where her stylist could tell her how beautiful she was as he went to work. The bitch had a great body, Angela thought, and she looked fantastic in that skirt. There was a hot, twisted feeling in Angela's stomach. It had been there since Conrad dropped her. Rage. It made her want to kick and scratch and bite. Kill something. What made these people think they were so much better than everyone else?

The receptionist returned to the front. She looked down her badly reconstructed nose at Angela and said, "Yes?"

"I'm here for a wash and blow dry." Angela wanted to remind this child to respect her elders but she just smiled.

"With who?" The receptionist actually yawned but failed to cover her mouth.

"Doesn't matter," Angela said. She wanted to kick in the woman's capped teeth but instead gave her most ingratiating smile. "Whoever."

"No appointment?" The receptionist looked at Angela with true surprise. "You just, like, stopped by?"

Angela smiled as sweetly as she could and nodded. Where did this idiot with the dry skin, cut-rate rhinoplasty and overly processed hair get off having attitude? She could wear the clothes and pile on the make-up but Angela could see, she could smell, that this little floozy came from the same nowhere place that Angela did.

"We are booked for weeks ahead of time." The receptionist tapped her fingernails on the appointment book. Metallic-blue manicure. Chipped. "It takes months to get in even if you have a connection. I mean, I guess I could put you down on a waiting list but don't hold your breath."

Angela looked around the room. There had to be sixty-five people working here. "You're telling me there isn't some assistant who could wash and dry my hair? Some apprentice?"

The receptionist chewed her gum and shrugged her shoulders. "Sorry."

Angela leaned in close. She could smell stale garlic beneath the mint gum. "I'd like to speak to your manager."

The girl took a step back and folded her arms across her chest. "I'm the manager and I'm telling you we don't have anyone who can work on you today or probably ever." She smiled. "There's a Fantastic Sam's down on Pico. I'm pretty sure they take *walk-ins*."

⸻

Judith happened to glance in the mirror when Graziano rushed off for her mint tea. She saw that Chantal was talking to that woman of Conrad's, looked like some kind of altercation. What on earth was she doing here? On a schoolteacher's salary? The girl caught her eye and waved. Now she was heading over.

"Mrs. Wentworth." She grabbed Judith's hand and shook it. "Angela Simms." Then she leaned in for a double-cheek kiss.

Judith sat perfectly still waiting for the contact to end. Who did she think she was? Conrad already dumped her; there was no need for this charade.

"I had such a lovely time at your house." Angela plopped down in the chair at the next station. "Did you get my note?"

"Yes." Judith certainly had not received a note. "Thank you."

Chantal came over. "Everything all right, Mrs. Wentworth?"

"Fine, dear."

Chantal lingered a moment. She clearly didn't like this woman anymore than Judith did, but what could one do?

Chantal touched Judith on the shoulder. "Let me know if you need anything." She walked back to the front desk.

"I was telling Conrad," Angela said. "Next time, we've got to do it at our house. Has he mentioned my roasted duck with beet garnish? It's one of his favorites. I know duck is rich and you obviously are so careful with what you eat, but once in a while you've got to splurge. Don't you think? It just melts in your mouth."

Graziano returned with the tea and Angela jumped out of her chair. "Angela Simms. Conrad's girlfriend." She took Graziano's hand and held it in both of hers. "Mrs. Wentworth has the most beautiful hair I've ever seen. The color is perfection. Conrad suggested I come in and talk to you about doing my hair."

Judith was speechless. Conrad didn't have a clue where Judith and Becky had their hair done. Conrad didn't notice women's hair. Graziano preened like he always did when someone paid attention to him or gave him the slightest compliment. Flattery shut down all his other senses and so he missed the look Judith was sending out. He missed her signals all together.

"Do you have my tongs?" Judith said. She watched the woman closely. You could always tell when people like this were lying.

"I'm sorry, what?" Angela's body stayed relaxed indicating probable truth.

"My silver tongs," Judith said. "Didn't Conrad mention them?"

"He did. I searched everywhere. You still haven't found them?"

"No." Judith wasn't completely sure. A trained liar could get away with murder.

Angela shook her head in sympathy then turned to Graziano and said,

"Any chance of me getting an appointment?"

"Of course." Graziano reached up and ran his finger through Angela's hair. "Anything for the Wentworths. You look like a young Judith." He turned to Judith. "Doesn't she?"

"Please," Angela said. "I'm no where near as beautiful as Judith. But thank you. That girl at the desk said you were booked up for months."

"Nonsense." Graziano turned and yelled across the room. "Chanty, find a place for Angela this week. Cut and color."

Chantal nodded but did not meet Angela's gaze.

"Great." Angela hugged Graziano. "I'll let you guys get to work." She bent and kissed Judith on the cheek. "Mrs. Wentworth, I'll have Con call and set up that dinner. We have a big announcement to make."

"Really?" Graziano said.

Angela giggled.

Judith heard a ringing sound in her ears. What on earth was this woman, this bloodsucking floozy, up to?

Graziano hugged Angela. "Want to whisper it in my ear?"

"Can't." Angela laughed. "Don't want to ruin the surprise." She winked at them and walked to the front desk where she paused and said something to Chantal, something that made Chantal flinch. Then she walked out the door.

"Do you know?" Graziano said.

Judith tried for her most neutral look and shook her head.

"Sounds like an addition to the family," Graziano said as he began to comb her out. "Lovely woman. You must be so happy. Why haven't I heard about her before?"

What Graziano wanted, what nourished his soul, was gossip. The slightest hint of a scandal would send him into a frenzy. He could flit around the room, going from station to station like an oversized bumblebee, and have a story spread in the time it took to get your hair washed. So Judith smiled. She would rather die than to let on that Angela Simms was a problem. A threat. A possible scandal.

8

Honey Carries On

*H*oney spent most of the morning vomiting. She'd felt thirsty but every time she drank a glass of water it worked like a trigger and her stomach would heave.

"Mommy?" Kimmy stood in the bathroom doorway staring at Honey who was kneeling by the toilet.

"Baby, go back to bed." Honey retched and some bile came up, burning her throat.

Kimmy started to cry.

"No, no baby. Don't cry." Honey tried to stand but another wave of sickness forced her to her knees. She threw up then wiped her mouth on the back of her hand. "Mommy's got the flu but it's okay. Everything's okay."

"Miss Angela said you had the flu last night." Kimmy's voice was shrill. "She promised you'd be all better this morning."

"You saw Angela?" Honey's body flashed hot with panic.

"When she got me from Mrs. Rappaport's. She wouldn't let me see you. Said you were sleeping." Kimmy started to cry again. "She's mean."

Honey forced herself up off the floor and hugged her daughter. The relief she should have felt was overridden by the hangover. God, she was sick. Her whole body shook as she stood there and held Kimmy. How was she supposed to be a mother when she felt like this? Why did everything have to be so hard? Her body temperature kept fluctuating and suddenly she was cold.

"Tell you what." Honey released Kimmy and turned her around. "Let's get in my bed and watch cartoons all day." She guided Kimmy down the hallway to the bedroom.

It turned out that barbecued potato chips and Dr. Pepper had an incredibly medicinal affect on Honey's hangover and as she lay there in bed watching the third episode of *Dora the Explorer* on Nickelodeon, she felt her body coming back to life. They would move. It was the only solution. She never wanted to see Angela again, she hated this city. There had to be better places and she would find one. She'd done it once under far worse circumstances, she could do it again.

Honey rolled over, so her back was against Kimmy's, and put a pillow over her head. She could see herself, that young girl all those years ago, sitting there in that truck behind the racks of bread and rolls.

There had been no plan B. If they caught her, her life would be over. Her stepfather would come into her bed every night. Her mother would look on approvingly. Honey's body had been numb with adrenaline and she felt herself shaking as she sat in the back of that truck. No tears. She didn't have the luxury of tears anymore. This horror had gutted her and left her completely defenseless. She rocked and rocked trying not to think. Then she stopped moving and held her breath as she heard someone load something into the back. Please God, please God, please God. The door shut. It was completely black and silent. The engine started. And in that blackness, as the truck pulled away, she allowed herself to hope.

"Mommy." Kimmy shook Honey's shoulder. "I'm just gonna go to the bathroom. Be right back."

When Jack opened the truck doors and saw her, he looked for a long moment before he spoke. "Wait here," he said. "Don't move and don't make any noise."

Honey didn't know why she trusted him. She couldn't remember a man in her life worthy of trust. But something about his face, his beautiful eyes, was kind. And anyway, she didn't really have a choice.

He went and got his pickup truck. He helped her get in the passenger side and told Honey to crouch on the floor then he covered her with a blanket. Honey never said a word. She didn't tell him she was running away. She didn't say why. He just seemed to know and he wanted to help her. Honey could feel that he was good.

They drove to his apartment. He gently took her arm, guided her into the building and up the steps. It was a nice place, a bedroom, small living room with a kitchenette. Honey remembered being surprised by how neat and clean everything was. Jack sat her down at the table and made her a turkey sandwich. He didn't ask if she was hungry, he just knew. When she'd finished, after he'd taken her plate and washed it, he sat opposite her and asked her name.

"You're running," he said. His voice was so kind. "You sure you want to go?"

Honey nodded. It was the one thing she was absolutely sure of.

"Then we're gonna have to get you some clothes. People don't wear old fashioned prairie dresses like that in the real world." He stood. "I don't suppose you've got any money?"

Honey shook her head. The whole concept of money wasn't something she'd given much thought.

Jack studied her. His manner changed slightly. "How old are you, anyway?"

With that question, Honey's survival instinct took over. She knew instinctively that this man would not want the responsibility of a fifteen-year-old girl. A child.

"I'm eighteen and a half." Honey's voice cracked. She cleared her throat, looked him in the eye and said forcefully, "My stepfather wanted me to be his fifth wife. My stepbrothers abused me.

My mother stood by and watched. I want a new life and I'm willing to work hard for it."

That was enough for Jack. He went out and bought her two pairs of jeans and a couple of blouses. Honey wondered how he figured out her size, but that was the kind of thing Jack always seemed to know. He could look at her and figure out exactly what she needed.

Kimmy climbed back into the bed and Honey took the pillow off her head.

"Can I have another soda, Mommy?"

"Sure baby." Honey didn't normally let Kimmy drink soda. "Get me one too."

It was the kindness Honey remembered most. The way he anticipated her needs. She almost never had to ask for things those first few months but Jack always knew what she wanted. He'd make her breakfast in the mornings before he went to work and then she spent the day watching TV. The commercials, the soap operas and the talk shows painted a picture of a life she'd never imagined, ugly but real. It was a world where people were jealous and angry and deceitful but it was the people themselves and not God who decided the consequences. People cheated on each other. They lied and they stole. Children ran away or self-destructed. Drugs. Alcohol. A lot of sex—talked about on TV but not really shown. Money. These were the triggers for disaster on those long afternoon shows. People lusted after each other's spouses. They envied the rich neighbor. They hid deep and ugly secrets. And with each installment of heartache and misery, Honey started to feel that maybe her life wasn't so weird after all. Yes, she'd come from a perverted universe but now she was a new resident in an equally distorted world. With each *General Hospital*, Honey felt her confidence grow. She could live out here. She could become one of these people. There really wasn't much difference between them and her. Life was going to be okay.

Jack usually got home around 6:00. He always brought dinner. Sometimes it was hamburgers and French fries but Jack didn't like junk food and, so just as often, he cooked. The idea of a man in the kitchen was ridiculous to Honey. She'd tried to take over but Jack seemed to like cooking and truthfully, he was better at it. He made simple things, broiled steaks, baked potatoes, salads, but his food was the best Honey ever tasted.

Honey washed the dishes and kept the house clean. Her mother had trained her well. She was good at scrubbing and dusting and vac- uuming. Thinking of how spotless she kept that apartment gave Honey a pang of anxiety. Why didn't she keep her own place in order? Why did she allow dishes to pile up and the floor to go unmopped? What happened to that young girl who took pride in doing a job well? All that would change. They would move and start fresh.

Kimmy came back with two more cans of Dr. Pepper. She handed them over for Honey to open then slid under the covers for more TV. Honey took a sip of her soda then put the pillow back over her head and closed her eyes.

The sex didn't start until much later, weeks after she'd moved in. Jack sometimes gave her back rubs after dinner or he'd massage her feet. She'd never been touched like that, gently and with kind- ness. He never asked her to do anything and it was Honey who ini- tiated the first kiss. He was lying on the couch taking a nap. He looked so beautiful, lying there with his eyes closed, so vulnerable. Honey kneeled next to the couch, leaned over and lightly brushed her lips across his. She kissed his eyelids and his cheeks. She hadn't known that she was going to do these things, her body just took over and some buried instinct directed her. Jack opened his eyes and smiled. He sat up and brought Honey up on the couch with him and kissed her. It was slow, and long and it gave Honey's body time to fill with longing and pleasure. It was a kiss she would never forget.

9

Norman is Not Going Back

*Y*ou? You're the village idiot. You're an insular, corn-fed bigot. You, who has never ventured beyond the perimeter of the white picket fence, are you really going to lecture me on the dos and don'ts of drinking? Hazards of mixing? Try and offer a life lesson while feeling smug about your superior sense of well-being? Listen, guppy face, I am the foremost authority in the field of abuse and recovery. Your helpful hints are like throwing pebbles at a battleship. I can't hear you.

I'm coating my stomach with Cozy Shack vanilla pudding. It comes in a six-pack, lasts forever in the refrigerator. Monochromatic foods after a night like that one. Milk. Pure whipped butter. I know, I know, the dangers of dairy. Well let me tell you something, puka shell, you get behind an eight-hour night with crystal (methamphetamine, pea brain), and you're going to be begging for maternal sustenance. I'd suck it right out of a baby bottle if there was one on hand, nipple and all. White food is step one in my program for recovery. Make a note.

Dr. Rosenblatt? You will be forced to leave if you mention his name again. Don't even bring it up. I will only say that I'm not interested in neuro-linguistic programming or the suppression of my fight or flight instinct. The whole thing is totally irrelevant and he's a fool, albeit an earnest fool. Oh yeah, the good doctor rolled up his sleeves, got out his tool box and put on his hard hat. He offered himself up as a hero, someone upon whom I could model my behavior. He stroked my inner child, balanced my right and left brain and concentrated positive energy on the enneagram of personality. There were foot rubs under the guise of reflexology. Pressure points. He proposed scream therapy as the route to self-actualization. But how could a man like that ever hope to understand an individual of my caliber? Hopeless. No, it was a complete waste of my valuable time and the therapy has unequivocally been terminated.

Now that I have lined my stomach with creamy white freshness I can proceed to step two. Watch and learn. This is the secret to success and it's one word: Cheetos. The body is dehydrated and in desperate need of salt—that's one reason for Cheetos. But, you might ask, can't one find salt in a wide variety of snacks? True. But Cheetos have a unique chemical composition that works with your metabolism and quickly breaks down the toxins in your body. It's the only food in the world that has these properties. I've tried to get the recipe, so I could replicate it here in my kitchen, but that information is highly classified. So, I will now devour this entire bag of Cheetos. Just one bite and I'm feeling better already.

He's an M.D., you say? You offer up his medical credentials as evidence of his competence? Let me tell you something, any idiot can go to medical school; it's simply a matter of memorization. But I'm going to surprise you here when I say that I think Dr. Rosenblatt is actually a very competent doctor for a certain type of person. He is uniquely qualified to treat most of the shortsighted, shallow thinking, morons that inhabit this earth. He is perfect for my sister, perfect for her entire family.

The final step of my cure is a sixteen-ounce glass of Dr. Pepper. Prune juice, no prune juice—not important. The interaction of Dr. Pepper with Cozy Shack pudding and Cheetos acts as a cleansing agent. Dr. Pepper, a quick nap, and I'll be as good as new, better than new. I'm going to sleep now. It's time for you to leave.

10

Monica and Joey
One-on-One

"I do talk to you."

"As if you like me, Joey."

"This is stupid."

"Remember rule number three? 'Family first'."

"Trying to make me puke?"

"If we can convince them we've grown closer, like happy, happy siblings, then maybe we can stop going."

"Mom needs it."

"I'm not talking about Mom. She's going to be in therapy for the rest of her life. Just us. I'm getting along with Dad really well. You are too. So all we have to do is show that we're good and that'll be it."

"What about Mom?"

"Huh?"

"We're not getting along with her."

"Nobody gets along with her. But they can't blame us for that. All we have to worry about is each other."

"Is Mom ever going to get better?"

"She's not insane. She's just a bitch."

"Will that get better?"

"Do you want to keep going to Dr. Rosenblatt? Cause if you do just say so and I'll stop wasting my time."

"No. I just wish Mom wasn't so..."

"Some people are naturally angry. It's not our fault."

"She makes it feel like it is, though."

"Maybe you should keep seeing Dr. Rosen-face."

"Shut up. I hate him."

"So start talking to me. Let's pretend like we're friends and then we'll be free."

11

***

Just Paul and Becky

***

$\mathcal{P}$aul and Becky were waiting to see Dr. Rosenblatt. This was their first visit without the kids and Paul felt nervous but also excited. Problems needed to be addressed—that was the bottom line. No secrets, no hiding. He knew he wasn't giving his wife what she needed but felt confident that if they could just identify what was missing, he could fill that gap. He could make Becky happy. He would. He must.

Becky was a reluctant patient. The appointments made her grumpy. She thought Dr. Rosenblatt looked like Ralph Nader, and Becky hated democrats, liberals. And there was no denying that they'd gotten off on the wrong foot with that first visit. But things were better at home, the kids were better, and so she continued to show up.

The door opened and Dr. Rosenblatt invited them in. It was a little awkward without the children. Should they take their regular seats? Should they share the three new things they discovered they liked about each other this week or was that an exercise for the family as a group? Would they use the talking stone for just the two of them?

Dr. Rosenblatt asked them to sit on the couch. He encouraged them to sit close so they could hold hands. Becky was never much of a hand holder but things were changing fast and who knew what might happen?

"Go ahead, Becky. Take Paul's hand." Dr. Rosenblatt settled back into his chair. "Touch is a very important element in the human experience. I'm sure you both know that."

Becky's hand felt boney, almost cold. Paul was surprise by the dryness of her skin, seemed like she was constantly applying some kind of lotion. Shouldn't she be softer?

"Today I hope we can begin to explore the more intimate side of your relationship," Dr. Rosenblatt said. "I'd like to discuss your sex life, the way you both feel about romantic relations and what you might want to improve."

Becky let out a loud sigh. Paul could feel her whole body tense.

"I know Becky, this can be a bit uncomfortable at first." Dr. Rosenblatt smiled. "If it helps, I'll tell you that I've been married for fifteen years to a wonderful woman but we've experienced our share of ups and downs. I've sat in your spot many times and frankly the couples counseling and sex therapy has saved my marriage more than once."

"I don't want to do this." Becky yanked her hand away from Paul, pulled her knees into her chest and locked her arms around her shins. "There's nothing wrong with our marriage. We came here 'cause of the kids."

"Look at your body language Becky," Dr. Rosenblatt said. "You're indicating that this is in fact an area of some concern. I see anger. Frustration. Sadness. Embarrassment."

"It's okay." Paul reached over and scratched Becky behind the ear then remembered that she hated that. He patted her on the shoulder. "I love you."

"Becky, I want you to put your head in Paul's lap." Dr. Rosenblatt got out of his chair and came over to the couch. He gently pulled Becky's arms apart and helped her uncurl. "That's right. I want you to just relax in your husband's lap. Maybe even close your eyes. We're all friends here. You're safe."

Becky curled into the fetal position and Dr. Rosenblatt removed her shoes then covered her with a throw blanket. Paul didn't really know what role he played here. He certainly didn't want to do anything wrong.

"Paul, I want you to gently massage Becky's temple." Dr. Rosenblatt leaned over and, with his middle and index fingers, gently rubbed Paul's right temple. "Like that. It will help Becky to relax."

Paul began massaging Becky's temple as Dr. Rosenblatt went around the room lighting candles. He dimmed the lights and then returned to his chair.

"Let's all close our eyes, shall we?"

Paul looked down and saw that Becky had her eyes squeezed shut as if in anticipation of some terrible calamity. Paul closed his eyes and hoped for the best.

"Now hum with me." Dr. Rosenblatt made a humming noise, not like a song, just a single sustained note. "Hmmmmmmmmmm-mmmmmmmmmmmm."

Paul felt a little shy, he'd never been much of a singer, but he tried to match Dr. Rosenblatt's pitch.

"Louder, Paul. From your diaphragm."

Paul forced himself to hum louder. Becky wasn't joining in.

"Becky, I need to hear from you. The humming is a way for us to release our tension. We'll bring it out into the room and let it float away like smoke. Hum Becky, Hum." Dr. Rosenblatt hummed again. Louder. Then Becky joined in. "Good Becky. Paul, don't stop rubbing her temples. Good."

They hummed for three or four minutes, long enough for Paul's throat to start feeling dry. Ever since that surgery for his snoring, dryness had been a problem but he wasn't going to complain. They had much bigger fish to fry.

"And stop."

Dr. Rosenblatt told Becky to roll over onto her back and asked Paul to delicately outline the contours of her face with his fingertips. They were supposed to keep their eyes shut but Paul kept sneaking peeks at Becky. She still had her eyes squeezed shut and didn't look in the least bit relaxed.

"How does it feel, Becky?" Dr. Rosenblatt said. "Do you like how Paul is touching you?"

"It feels like bugs are crawling on me," she said. "It makes me want to claw my face."

Paul took his hand away and felt himself blush with shame. This was the problem, right here. He had no idea how to approach his wife. He didn't have a clue how to satisfy her. What did she want from him?

"Sit up, Becky. Open your eyes," Dr. Rosenblatt said. "We're going to try something else. Everyone is different. Every person has a different definition of what's pleasurable. There's no good or bad, right or wrong. We just need to find your comfort zone."

Paul felt a tremendous sense of gratitude. Someone was finally going to sort this out.

Dr. Rosenblatt moved the coffee table away from the couch and told Becky to sit on the floor between Paul's legs. Then he told Paul to put his hands on her shoulder and to massage her muscles.

"How's that feel, Becky?" Dr. Rosenblatt said.

"Good." Becky seemed to be relaxing.

Paul dug his thumbs into her stringy muscles and manipulated her back with his palms.

"Could it feel better?" Dr. Rosenblatt said.

"Yeah, maybe."

"How, Becky, how? Tell Paul how to make it better."

"Harder."

"Use his name, Becky. Say Paul's name."

"Harder, Paul. Do it harder."

And so Paul dug his fingers in to his wife's boney shoulders. She felt so fragile that at first he was afraid of the pressure she seemed to be asking for. But the harder he squeezed and pushed the more relaxed she became. She started to moan and Paul found himself using all his strength to knead away her tension.

12

❦

When Lunch Doesn't Sit Well

❦

*G*us sat in the men's lounge with his martini and a set of
dominoes. It was 11:30 and most of his friends were still out
on the golf course. Normally that's where Gus would have been
but this morning he just hadn't felt like getting out of bed and
when he did finally drag himself up for breakfast, he'd missed his
Friday tee time. He wasn't sick. In fact, Judith had insisted he have
a checkup just the other day and everything was fine. But he was
tired a lot and the things that had once sounded so appealing no
longer held his interest.

David Halliburton had been a great domino player. God, that
man had a mind for numbers; he almost never lost. Luck and skill
had made him club champion five years running. Even up to the
end, when he'd stopped playing golf and didn't really have the
energy to stay much past lunch, David would be there, five days a
week, cleaning everyone's clock.

Losing David was a big one. Sure other members had gotten
sick and died. Crawford Eagan had that stroke. Nat Cushing
dropped dead in this very lounge of a heart attack. John Mollant
finally succumbed to colon cancer and just last week Charlie
Henson was diagnosed with pancreatic cancer—one of the fastest

and worst. Losing all those friends had been hard but it was David who really hit home. David was Gus' best friend, the one he'd shared his entire life with, the memories, the childhood. David had been there since childhood, playing on the Santa Monica beach as boys, body surfing in the summer and later lifeguarding.

Gus reached for his drink. When had the tremor started? A year ago? At first it had been so subtle, and so infrequent, that he attributed it to a few too many drinks the night before. But gradually he noticed that the tremor, that slight shaking of the hand, was with him most of the time. Had Judith noticed? Probably. Must be why she insisted on the checkup. The doctor said it might be related to the drinking—hell, he said it probably was, but he also said that some people just develop a shaky hand as they age. It could all be a function of getting older.

Gus ate the olives and studied the lunch menu that hadn't changed in over thirty years. He wasn't hungry today. That was unusual. In fact Gus just didn't feel well. Tired. He reached for his check, signed his name, finished off his drink and stood. He'd go home. Hopefully Judith would be out and he could crawl into bed for a nap.

13

Rosa Gets an Ear Full

The Missus, she is mad. Throwing one of her little tantrums where the world is the enemy and the problems are all my fault. I've learned to stay away when she gets like this. Pretend to scrub a nasty stain in the sink or clean the toilets over again. But poor Carmen, she's not so smart. She walked right up to the Misses and asked, "Do you want some tea, Missus?" And the Missus, she slaps Carmen with her ugly words. "If I want something Carmen, I will ring for it. Don't you have something better to do than wasting my time?"

Now Carmen is crying in the butler's pantry and the Missus is up in her room with the pig. These people don't have any idea what it is to have a real problem. I'd like to show them, someday. Maybe I will. What they don't know, and what no one is ever going to tell them, is that the vent in the bedroom is like a speaker into the laundry room downstairs. I can stand by the washer and hear everything they say. Usually it's too boring, her barking about nothing and him with his snorts and belches. Sometimes they fight. I've never heard them have sex. No, I don't bother to listen most of the time. I've got better things to do. But today, why not? Maybe I can make Carmen laugh with a funny story.

"Do you think she could be pregnant?"

"God, I hope not."

"Conrad hates beets, you know."

"I didn't know."

"You had lunch with him last week. He say anything?"

"We talked about the market."

"I think she followed me, August."

"Come on."

"She's after something."

"Maybe she really liked your hair."

"Did you see the way she looked around the house at the dinner."

"Nope."

"Like she was taking inventory. Shopping."

"He says they broke up."

"So you did talk about her."

"Not really. Just that."

Pause.

"Can you check this spot on my neck?"

"What?"

"This mole."

"I don't see anything."

"Of course you do. It's a brown mole. I can feel it."

"Okay. So?"

"Does it look any different?"

"How the hell would I know? I've never seen it before."

"That's what I'm worried about. I think it's bigger. Is it black and mottled?"

"I don't know, Judith. Go to the goddamn doctor if you're worried."

"Are there any hairs growing out of it? That's a good sign if there are. Did you know?"

"I can't see anything."

"Lean in. Please."

"Looks okay."

"You've been drinking."

"No."

Pause.

"I can smell it on you. It's one o'clock in the afternoon and you've been drinking. Honestly August, don't you have anything better to do with your day? Not to mention the health risks."

"Cork it, Judith. I had one glass of white wine. Big deal."

"You know they've proven that excessive drinking does cause cancer and I'd say getting drunk at lunch and dinner seven days a week constitutes excess."

"Is there any setting other than NAG?"

"You're starting to get one of those W. C. Fields noses. You want that? August?"

Rustling.

"Where do you think you're going? We need to deal with this Angela situation."

"Call Conrad."

"He's in Geneva. I tried."

Door slams.

"She's obviously after money."

Silence.

"And I'm absolutely positive that she's the one who took my tongs."

Knocking on the door.

"August."

Shower starts.

Footsteps pound down the hallway.

—◆—

Uh-oh. Here she comes. Time to hide. She'll be breathing fire because her husband, the pig, is locked away in the shower and there's no place for her to put the rage. Maids are dumpsters for the rich. Angry? Disappointed? Sad? Unload it on us. Yell, scream, say whatever you want. We'll take it, that's what you pay us for. We clean up messes, make your life feel a little better, a little cleaner. It's our job.

14

Paul and Becky Explore

aul and Becky made real progress in their couples therapy. Dr. Rosenblatt had helped them see that there was really no area too strange or embarrassing to explore. At first Becky was very hesitant to participate in this aspect of the treatment. Sex with Paul had never been a real priority. In fact, sex had never held much interest at all for Becky. She found that she was most satisfied when alone, perhaps in the bathtub, or in front of a mirror after a good massage, thinking about herself and how she was admired by those around her. "Oh Becky, you have such a beautiful body." "Oh Becky, your breasts look so young." She had sexual feelings but she didn't necessarily have them when anyone else was in the room. It was more of a private thing for her, a solo thing. Dr. Rosenblatt said he could fix that, he could help her enjoy sex with Paul, if she'd just trust him and follow his instructions.

Paul was more than game. He'd always found his wife to be beautiful, and he was tremendously attracted to her, but with Dr. Rosenblatt's help, he was able to admit that there were times that he found her indifference to be off-putting. He wished that she wasn't so cold.

They'd started with simple massage, the touching and exploring of each other's bodies in a non-sexual way. Paul found that he liked to have his stomach rubbed in a circular motion and, once Becky talked him into waxing his torso, she didn't mind accommodating him. Becky discovered that it felt good to have her arms pulled straight back behind her body so that her hands touched. She told Paul that it was the stretching across her chest that she liked. What she didn't say was that it hurt a little bit and that the tiny bit of pain was enormously relaxing. They both reported their progress to Dr. Rosenblatt who was very pleased and gave them permission to advance.

The next phase of therapy involved massage in a sexual context. Intercourse was still strictly forbidden. Nipples, breasts, buttocks, scrotum, penis, labia, clitoris, anus, perineum, all these areas were to be explored with the gentle touch of hands and copious amounts of lubricant. The point was to learn each other's body while learning about one's self. Again, Paul found that his torso was tremendously responsive. He liked to have Becky start on his stomach then work her way down to the pubic area. Again Becky was put off by the hair and so Paul waxed his entire body, including the hair on his scrotum—a terribly painful procedure. Once the hair was gone, Becky was much more attentive.

Becky found pleasure through penetration. Because they were restricted in what they could do in this phase of the program, because Paul was not allowed to enter his wife, they improvised with household items and store bought toys. Then one day Becky brought home a variety of monstrously large zucchini from the farmer's market. She spent a good deal of time washing her purchases, even though they were organic, and then secreted them up to the bedroom. At first Paul had been put off by his wife's request but when he saw the longing in Becky's eyes, he acquiesced. He started with the smallest of the vegetables and was frankly shocked when he discovered how large Becky's appetite really was. But, as Dr. Rosenblatt constantly reminded them, there was no wrong or right, only pleasure.

At the week's end, they dutifully reported back to Dr. Rosenblatt who was very pleased. He insisted they describe, in great detail, the highlights of their exploration, focusing especially on Becky's success. It was good work, he said, very good work indeed. Dr. Rosenblatt gave his blessing and granted permission for them to move on to the next phase: Intercourse.

15

Assault on the Inner Sanctum

$\mathscr{B}$ecky pulled her car up to the valet station, grabbed her liter bottle of Fiji water, took the ticket from the attendant and rushed inside without bothering to say hello or thank you. Becky was in a hurry. The 4:00 class was about to start and being late meant a spot at the back of the class where Rico's fine young face and body would be obscured by thirty other ladies vying for his attention. This was The Yoga and Spinning Institute of Brentwood and competition was fierce. They only hired the most attractive of instructors who offered exquisite motivation by way of suggestive smiles, full body hugs and, for the truly outstanding student, the occasional pat on the bum. Here you could find Brentwood matrons sitting on a stationary bikes seven days a week, pedaling as fast as they possibly could in an effort to escape the dreaded cellulite that threatened every woman's back end. Or if you came on the odd numbered hours 9, 11, 1, 3, 5 or 7, you would find those same matrons twisting and honing their bodies through the vigorous yet enlightening pursuit of yogic perfection.

Becky signed in at the front desk and rushed to Studio 7. Just as she'd suspected the front three rows of bikes were completely taken, mostly by regulars, but there were a couple of newcomers, one of them in the very first row. There should be a law against that: new people should have to stay in the back until they establish themselves. Becky had been attending this same 4:00 class with Rico for over a year. Fourteen months to be exact. It was the highlight of her day and frankly she was probably responsible for his huge popularity. She talked about Rico's class to everyone who would listen, even brought her mother along when he was first starting out so there'd be more students. That's loyalty. They ought to reserve a bike for her. Would it kill Rico to go out of his way? Everything she'd done and especially after that nice Christmas present she gave him? Becky climbed on a bike in the forth row and pulled on her riding gloves. She would have a word with him, give him a piece of her mind.

The woman on the bike in front of her turned. "Becky?"

Who was this?

"Angela," she said. "Conrad's girlfriend." She got off her bike, gathered up her stuff and came back to Becky's row.

"Oh. Yeah." Becky considered switching bikes. What did she care about being rude to one of Conrad's women? But before she could make her move Magda Birtch, a regular, swooped in and grabbed the spot.

Angela climbed on next to Becky. "What a nice coincidence."

"It's an advanced class, you know." Becky checked her watch. 4:03. Rico was late. "Mostly hill work. Real fast intervals."

"Great." Angela pulled on her riding gloves and tested the resistance settings on the bike. "Saw your mom at Faberge's earlier today. Graziano does you too, right?"

"For years," Becky said. What the hell was this poser doing at Faberge's?

"I've got an appointment later this week," Angela said. "Can't wait to see what he does with my color. Your mom insists he's the best and you both look so great." She cleared her throat and smiled. "Listen, Con and I are having your parents for dinner when he gets back from Geneva. Why don't you and Paul come?

Becky looked at Angela. No way. There was absolutely no

chance that this girl, this average little nothing, this conniving bitch, this *preschool teacher*, had made it past the farewell family dinner. She had to be lying. Or maybe Conrad was losing his grip? Angela and Conrad, that made Becky smile. They deserved each other.

"We do a pretty mean duck," Angela said.

Rico finally arrived and walked to the front of the class, stopping here and there for the heartfelt kiss on the cheek. He didn't even notice Becky sitting in fourth row.

"What do you say?" Angela said. "We could make it early?"

Becky said. "I don't eat ducks."

16

What Does Norman Think?

The alarms are blasting, can you hear them? Warning, Warning, Warning. Interloper. Danger, Danger, Danger. Someone beneath us trying to step up. Man the turrets, load the cannons. Judith is having trouble with the drawbridge and August is offering virtually no help at all. It's a potential crisis with global ramifications. Level 5 alert. Conrad's girlfriend isn't crawling away with a broken heart and crushed spirit, never to be heard from again. NO. Angela Simms is fighting back. She wants her piece of the pie, a big slice, a la mode. And even though we own the bakery, we don't offer handouts. Oh, what shall we do? Is this the beginning of the end of the Wentworth Empire? Becky just called hysterical; the encroacher showed up at the exercise studio offering a duck dinner. Pure evil. What is the solution? How will the Wentworth family survive this attack?

I haven't had a visit from Miss Angela Simms. She hasn't bothered to ascertain my day-to-day routine. She hasn't made an appearance at Joe to Go, my coffee spot. I don't see her lurking in the weight room of Hardbodies Gym in West Hollywood. She's not lunching at Ken's Deli or having drinks at the Friendship Bar. No, she's not making any effort at all to contact me. I should be hurt. Am I not also a full-blooded Wentworth? Do I not have value as a bargaining chip in her complicated plan? It could be seen as the ultimate insult, one from which I might not recover if I were a weaker sort of soul. I could withdraw in anger and bitterness, vow to reject this thoughtless harlot in the way of my kinfolk. I could potentially turn violent at the indignity of the situation. But, as you so well know, I exist on an elevated plane, far above the petty concerns of my oh-so-small-minded relatives. No, I will not reject Angela Simms. I will find her and I will embrace her. I applaud her spirit and her courage. I will aid her in battle and see to it that she is triumphant in this heroic effort.

17

If You Wax It, He Will Come

At the beginning, the woman has all the power and it's on the first date that you want to lay the groundwork for future operations. Get through dinner quickly and head back to the house, make a beeline for the bedroom and get busy. Men are helpless when it's new and strange, intoxicated by the smell of you. Pretend to have an orgasm right away just from kissing and rubbing back and forth against him. Be fairly vocal about it, he'll be amazed. Enthusiasm counts for a lot. Peel his clothes off and marvel at the size and beauty of his penis. If it's small, focus on the beauty part. Have another orgasm when he sticks his hand in your panties, try to work up a real sweat. Talk dirty about his amazing body and the way it makes you feel. Again, if the body isn't so great, focus on something like skin tone or color. Take him over to the bed and jump on board for a very animated ride then suddenly stop and walk around the room. Sit in a chair, play with yourself, legs wide apart so he can see you. Talk about his huge size, again. Have yet another orgasm (this one will probably be real since you're doing all the work). Come back to bed and slowly lower yourself down on top of him, but not all the way. Drive him crazy. Make him beg. He will be so, so grateful that you can probably get away with anything. Yeah, get what you need quick, on that first date, cause he's never going to want you this badly again.

I memorized the combination to the alarm system on that first night as we came in Conrad's front door. I just stood beside him and kissed his neck as he punched in the code. #-4-5-4-3-7-*. I'm good with numbers so there was no danger of forgetting but you might need to jot it down. Later I nabbed his keys on the way up the stairs to his bedroom. I just grabbed them and zipped them into the inner pocket of my purse. When it was time to take me home, he blamed himself for being forgetful and went off for his spare set. You see, I had my security plan in place right from the start.

It's a big house. Cold if you ask me. No homey touches, no knickknacks. Concrete and glass and leather with those godawful paintings. Francis Bacon was one fucked-up guy. Tortured souls being pulled apart in slow, bloody motion. Grays and blacks and dripping, meaty reds. Depressing. What's wrong with a nice landscape? A vase of flowers? Bowl of fruit? We're sending those paintings to his office, or selling them, once I get this all worked out.

There's a safe in the bathroom behind where he stores the towels. Probably a couple more located throughout the house. No, I don't have the combinations to those—even I'm not that good. It's okay though, there's plenty of stuff just lying around the house. Like what? Well, how about the copious supply of party favors? Cocaine? X? Quaaludes, believe it or not? Yeah, the guy's well stocked. He's got an assortment of medieval torture junk—or whatever you want to call it—the hoods, chains, stockade. I just know his lovely mother would be interested in that nice collection. But the thing that interests me most, the real reason I'm here, is his personal video collection. The guy's quite the cinematographer. I starred in several feature length films, alone and with my friend Alison. I was an enthusiastic supporter of Conrad's efforts and insisted we view our movie over and over. And thus his secret library was revealed to me. With a little begging and a lot of flattery I was able to talk him into showing me some of his earlier work and what do you know, some of those girls he so skillfully recorded are definitely not 18, a couple of them don't even look 14. So I'm here today to pick up the highlights. The D.A. would be interested in a special screening should the need arise, don't you think?

Is it dangerous for me to be sneaking around in his house? Naw. The maid's gone for the day and it won't get dark for at least another hour so I don't have to turn on any lights. No one's going to know. Except Conrad. Conrad will know. He gets back from his trip tonight. Conrad will come home and he'll find my panties on his pillow and my nice note.

Dear Con,

I borrowed a couple of movies. The twins, Alison and me, and that one with your friend's teenage daughter. What was her name? So pretty. I miss you and I can't wait till you get back. Maybe we can make a new film all our own.

Eternally Yours,
Angela

18

Wake Up, Jack

*J*ack was sick. He'd been driving around California, aimlessly, sleeping under the stars, smoking and drinking way too much. Now he had a cough and a fever. The sheets were damp with sweat and he alternated between hot and cold. Jack was thirsty but the refrigerator in his cheap motel room was broken. Warm beer didn't sound like a cure. His skull pounded. He kept thinking that if he could just take his head off and lay it on a cushion of soft pillows, he'd feel a lot better. If he got rid of his head, life would be so simple. Food, drink, sex, sleep, that's all his body would need. He wouldn't have to think about any of the bullshit. But he was stuck with his head and it was making his whole body miserable.

He coughed and the pressure made his eyes water. The tearing feeling in his chest made him wonder again about his lungs and their actual life span. He'd been smoking those hand-rolled cigarettes for close to twenty years now. No filter, no sissy shit for this man. His attitude had always been, *fuck it, when my time comes, I'll be ready to check out*. Live every moment. But lately doubt had been creeping in and enveloping his whole belief system like a dense fog pushing in from the dark cold ocean. Things weren't so clear to him now. What if this was cancer? He definitely wasn't ready to go yet. He'd spent his life drifting from one place to another leaving virtually no trace with the exception of a few hard feelings. Shouldn't there be something more? A reason.

Jack sat up and took some more aspirin for his headache. Sick or not, he had to make a plan. Honey was listed in the phone book. Her apartment wasn't too far from his shit-hole motel. All he had to do was pick up the phone. A simple call would tell him everything he needed to know. But Jack had been camping out in this room for three days now, sick with a flu that was probably brought on by doubt and fear. He hadn't been sick in years and now he couldn't shake this damn thing because his mind was using every ounce of energy in an effort to answer one stupid fucking question: What exactly is the right time to call someone and tell them your whole life has been a mistake? How do you start the conversation that ends with I'm sorry for ruining your life and will you please forgive me? In the course of those long days at the motel, Honey's flaws had fallen away one by one and now she stood high above his head on a marble pedestal. Honey was perfect. Who else in this world had loved him like she had? Who could kiss him with such tenderness and such heat? What woman had ever responded to him in bed as passionately as Honey had? There was no one else. She was his mate. They were meant to be. Jack put his head back down on the pillow and slept.

19

Honey

Honey called in sick and kept Kimmy home from school for an entire week. She'd told Gus she had a bad cough, terrible intestinal problems plus a very bad yeast infection. He'd gone away and hadn't bothered to check up on her. Kimmy was, at first, thrilled to stay home with her mother and watch TV. Soda, chips and cartoons. What could be better? But after four days, even Kimmy started to go a little crazy. Honey realized she couldn't really make a plan for the next step if she didn't first face her situation and deal with it. She needed to go to work. She needed to talk to Gus. She needed some time to plan out the escape. And so on Monday morning Honey got Kimmy ready and walked her the three blocks to the Happy Helpers Preschool.

Angela hadn't called since that night. Surely she was disgusted and Honey half expected to be turned away when they got to the school. On the walk, she had to stop several times, her body cringed and revolted every time a memory from that night slipped out.

"What's wrong, Mommy." Kimmy tugged on her arm.

"Suddenly you're in a hurry?" Honey smiled at Kimmy. "I thought you didn't like it there."

"I like snack time." Kimmy grabbed her hand and they started walking a little faster. "And Jell-O the Bunny. I miss Jell-O."

The red door was open and most of the children were already busy putting away stuff in their cubbies or playing in the sandbox. Honey took a deep breath, forced all thoughts from her head, and walked into the play yard with Kimmy. There, over by the lady-bug-themed swing set, stood Angela talking to one of the mothers.

⸺

Look who's doing the walk of shame? Poor Honey. I never would have suspected that dull little Mormon had so much fire in her. But now she's mortified. You should have been there. Talk about the dam breaking, fucking Niagara Falls. She was all over me. Kept saying she'd never done anything like that before but once I got her started, there was no stopping. Got to admit, it was pretty fun. We were at it for what seemed like hours until poor Honey started throwing up—that pretty much put an end to it. I'd almost consider a revisit, but it's too much work.

I definitely got what I needed from her, little thing has a memory like an elephant. Still, you never know when I might want to go back, check the Wentworth status.

⸺

Honey focused closely on getting Kimmy's sweater and lunch box stowed neatly in the cubby. If she didn't make eye contact with Angela, maybe Angela wouldn't notice her. She escorted Kimmy into the art room and got her busy with some crayons then headed for the back exit.

"Honey." Angela rushed over, grabbed her and pulled her into a tight hug and kissed her on the cheek. She whispered in her ear, "I've missed you."

Honey stepped back. She worked her face into what she hoped was a smile.

"I'm so glad Kimmy's back." Angela seemed so happy, like nothing bad had happened. "Cold again? The flu's been going around."

"The flu," Honey said. There were a couple of mothers, women Honey had never spoken to, headed in their direction. Honey prayed they needed Angela's attention and sure enough they came up with an apparently urgent message.

"Miss Angela," the tall dark-haired woman said. "Julian Speaks is telling a group of children that people can have 'sax' with dogs and his father is out there laughing."

Angela took off for the play yard and the two concerned mothers followed. Honey let herself out the back exit and headed for home.

20

Norman Getting to Know Angela

I've come to her house. Well, it's not actually a house. It's a *duplex*. Angela Simms lives in a duplex. Angela Duplex. Sounds French, doesn't it? Originally this was a single-family dwelling, a tract house, beige, probably built in the mid-seventies, and there's a straight path that leads from the sidewalk up to the house. It splits into a "Y" at the last possible moment and if you turn left you'll be at her front door. I don't know who lives on the right side. I rang the bell but no one answered. Then I put my ear to the door and thought I heard a parrot or Macaw screeching inside, but I can't be sure of that. There is no name on the mailbox.

Angela lives in 1304 "A". Nice how that works—A for Angela. Do you think the "A" had anything to do with her choice of dwellings? Perhaps subconsciously. There is no "B" in her name. Unless her middle name is Babette or Bijou or Blanch. (I'll make a note to check that.) She has a red front door. It's the exact same glossy red of the door at the preschool. From that tiny detail I ascertain that Miss Angela Duplex is a thrifty person, someone who watches her pennies and makes excellent use of a gallon of paint. (I have tremendous natural ability in this area, you know. I could have been a private investigator. I still might, plenty of time.)

The narrow walkway along the side of the house is where Angela keeps her trashcans but unfortunately yesterday was the pick-up so the cans are empty and there's no evidence to examine. A strong smell in this area is an indication of carelessness, messy spills and whatnot. Angela's obviously not vigilant about her garbage—or not vigilant enough. I'd scrub the whole walkway with bleach, wash the cans, and start over. Maybe I'll help her with that once we're friends.

It's a small backyard and she's got her side screened off with a solid, unpainted, redwood fence. There are little sharp pickets at the top of each board and the gate is locked from the inside. No, of course it didn't stop me. I climbed over but now I've got a nasty redwood splinter in the palm of my right hand. I'm torn between digging it out and leaving it alone. Redwood tends to get infected. On the other hand, the body does protect itself in amazing ways—at least my body does.

Look, Angela's got a Jacuzzi, a little four-seater. I've seen ones just like this advertised when I drive down the freeway around Carson and El Segundo. The tub is mounted impossibly high on a revolving pole; the whole thing spins in the sky so you'll be sure to notice. You've seen them too, at places like Spa World or Whirlpool Emporium. This Jacuzzi looks like one of the less expensive models, kind of flimsy. But as we've learned, Angela Duplex watches her pennies. Look, it's called the "X-Spa-Dition." I'll bet she's had plenty of adventures here.

As luck would have it, the sliding glass door is unlocked. Actually, I don't believe in luck. Things happen for a reason; at least they do in my world. The door is not secured because I was meant to enter this home. And even if it had been locked, I have a fair amount of experience with breaking and entering. Let's step inside, shall we? Smells good. See it there over in the corner? A Glade PlugIns. I'm guessing Rainshower or maybe Hawaiian Breeze. At least she had the good sense to stay away from the vanilla family—nothing worse.

Angela's living room is an over-crowded ode to mediocrity.

Cheap white coffee tables and matching bookshelves, woven throw-rugs and bright cotton pillows. A striped armchair almost clashes with the floral pattern of the two-seater sofas but somehow manages to pull the whole room together. Pottery Barn, Pier 1, IKEA, or maybe, maybe Restoration Hardware. Give me fifteen minutes and a computer and I'll hand you a definitive answer. At least she hasn't filled the place with embarrassing family heirlooms and bad antiques. My guess is that Miss Angela didn't keep many relics from her past.

Oh look, she's been to the County Museum gift shop and bought posters from several of the big shows. A nice bowl of pears—Cezanne before things got too crazy. Monet, of course. Manet. Seurat. Oh, she's going out on a limb here with this thin-faced Modigliani woman. Maybe Angela sees a resemblance? This is good news. She and I can talk about art, gush about water lilies and quality of light. It will be our common ground, a starting point.

Don't panic. Someone just unlocked her front door. Quickly, slide the glass door shut and follow me out the gate. She doesn't usually leave work until five but admittedly I've only had her under surveillance for forty-eight hours. Hurry. Don't make any noise. Now duck down as you go past the kitchen window. Yep, that's her car parked in front. Next time we'll visit in the morning when she's definitely at school. We won't make this mistake again.

21

Knock, Knock

$\mathcal{G}$us was a couple of minutes early and instead of using his key, he knocked. That was a surprise. Gus had never knocked before. Honey opened the door and saw him standing there with flowers. Flowers? Most of the gifts that Gus supplied were functional: Tempur-Pedic pillows for his neck, high count cotton sheets for his skin, the occasional bottle of vodka or bourbon that only he drank—Honey couldn't stand the stuff. But here, today, he was presenting her with a real gift. What the heck was going on?

"They're beautiful," Honey said. And they were, some kind of lily. "But I don't think I have anything to put them in."

Gus laughed and pulled from behind his back, a clear glass cylinder, plain but elegant. "I grabbed this from home." He handed her the vase. "Figured you might need it."

"Won't your wife . . ."

"Naw, we got tons of this kind of stuff." Gus took the flowers and headed towards the kitchen. "Got to cut the stems before you put them in water."

Honey followed Gus. He opened the kitchen drawer and pulled out a knife then sawed off the bottom two inches of the stems as she filled the vase with water.

"When they start to open," he said. "You want to pull these guys off." He put the flowers in the vase and demonstrated how to remove the end of the stamen. "Get them right away when the petals start to open otherwise you'll get pollen all over the place and it kind of ruins the look of the flowers." He carried the vase back out into the living room and sat it down on the coffee table.

"Thank you, Gus." Honey didn't know what to think. Who was this guy? Why was he being so nice? Lessons on flower arranging?

"It's the least I can do, Honey."

~

I love Honey, I really do, but I've got to get rid of her, move her somewhere far away. Angela Simms is a goddamn psycho and there is no reason why she shouldn't use Honey as a weapon against me, against the entire Wentworth family. Honey is a definite weakness in my defense. It's not going to be easy though. She's got a pretty good deal here, don't you think? I pay the rent, Kimmy's school. All she's got to worry about are the incidentals and how much can they be? Plus, Honey loves me. So it's complicated.

~

Judith parked her car halfway up the block. She'd seen August go into the butler's pantry and take that vase, not one of her better ones but it was expensive, very good quality glass. What on earth was he doing? He'd thought she was upstairs in the bath and so he slipped quietly from the house, probably thrilled that he got out undetected. Fool. There was very little that Judith didn't notice in the home, not much got by her. She grabbed her purse and keys and followed. First he'd stopped at The Woods, Twigs and Flowers. What on earth? That was *her* florist. Was he getting something for Judith? Not a chance. A sick friend? He would have mentioned that. In fact, he would have insisted that Judith take care of floral arrangements if it was for a friend. She parked behind a dumpster and waited in the parking lot of the dry cleaners next door while he went into the florist. It occurred to her that she could stop him. Just walk up and tell him to turn around. It was her chance to insist that he not do whatever he was considering, come home. They could go on as usual, no harm done, pretend it never happened. She would put that vase back in the pantry and everything would be fine. But when she saw August walk to his car carrying a huge bouquet of Casa Blanca lilies, her favorite flower, Judith knew that things had already gone too far. There was no turning back.

—

Honey took off her blouse. The sooner she got this over the better. Then she could talk to Gus about getting help. She was going to try extra hard in bed today, get him in a really good mood, then lay out her plan.

"Wait," Gus said. "Come sit on the couch first. Let's talk."

Honey dropped her blouse on the chair and sat next to Gus. Maybe he wanted to just look at her in her bra. You never knew what Gus wanted when he showed up. It was hard to anticipate what would turn him on on any given day.

"Honey," he said. "I know that you and Kimmy are very happy here." Gus took her hand and stroked her fingers, something he'd never done before. "The apartment, the neighborhood, walking distance to a great school. I know it must seem ideal to you."

Honey felt a panic rising in her body. What was he talking about? Had she ever said anything about being happy? Did she ever even smile when he was around? Not very often. But here he was outlining her great life, virtually making it impossible for her to contradict him. It was like Gus was sealing the windows and nailing shut the doors, getting ready to hold her prisoner in this world he'd help create.

—

Judith walked up the sidewalk towards the shoddy pink stucco building. She'd seen him mount the stairs and knock on the door of that first apartment. Who on earth would live in a place like this? One of the maids? Was August Wentworth seeing one of her maids? Judith did a quick inventory. Rosa was working at the house. Carmen had been vacuuming upstairs when Judith left. Blanca was helping reorganize the kitchen over at Becky's house today. No, her girls were all accounted for. And yet she couldn't think of anyone they knew who would come to a place like this. Not that it was dangerous, it was just...cheap. Tacky. Judith felt her body relax. There had to be a perfectly good explanation. She reached the stairs and, careful not to touch the filthy railing, made her way up to find her husband.

Honey looks cute sitting here in her bra, doesn't she? How am I ever going to find someone like her again? Face it, I'm an old man and the young girls aren't exactly beating a path to my door. Yes, of course I could pay for it, and I suppose you would say that I paid Honey for it, but that's not really true. She's different, a good kid. Good intentions. I trust Honey, I really do. And she cares about me, I can tell. We've developed something of a relationship, the two of us. It's going to be hard on her, hard on both of us, when she goes. But what can I do?

Honey let Gus play with her fingers. His hands were more clammy than usual, seemed like he was nervous about something. She kept waiting for him to continue talking but he just looked into her eyes.

"You okay?" she said.

"Fine." He put his hand on her cheek and held her chin. "You have lovely eyes, Honey. I never noticed before."

"Thanks, Gus." Honey leaned over and started to unzip his pants.

"I need to talk." He blew out a big breath. "We need to talk."

How's a guy supposed to think in a situation like this? Might be the last time for us. The last time ever. That's a very sad thought. And you know there are going to be tears, lots of tears, when I tell her. Poor thing, it's going to break her heart. See how much she wants it? She's not usually that enthusiastic about the blowjobs. Must be the flowers. Why didn't I use the whole flowers and candy approach earlier? Because I'm an idiot, that's why. She's got me unzipped and I'm reporting for duty, on time and ready for action. Five star salute. I'll tell her afterwards.

Gus put his hands behind his neck and leaned back on the couch. He was ready. Honey took a deep breath and went to work.

Judith stood outside the grimy white door of apartment #7. She knew she would have to knock eventually but she wasn't quite ready. Did she really want to know? Did it matter? She leaned in close and listened. Nothing. Maybe nothing was going on. Nonsense. She knew there was something. She'd always known there was something. It was sad and it was painful but that's just how men were, real men, and August was certainly a real man. It was biological, they couldn't help it. So why was she here now? What did this one really matter? She'd ignored so many others over the years, why not continue to turn a blind eye? Because he took her vase, that's why. How dare he take one of her things and give it to one of his strumpets. She wanted it back and she wanted her husband back too.

Judith raised her right hand and pounded on the door.

"Who's that?" Gus sat forward.

"Don't know." Honey sat up and wiped her mouth with the back of her hand. "Mrs. Rappaport? I'll go see."

"No. Finish." Gus guided Honey's head back down then leaned back. "Ignore it."

The pounding came again, this time more insistent. Honey ran through the list of possibilities. If it was Mrs. Rappaport, she would eventually go away, maybe slip a note under the door. If it was Mr. Sampson from next door, he'd come back later. But if it was the building manager, and he needed to check something in the apartment, and Honey didn't answer, there was a good chance that he'd just come barreling through the door.

"I've got to answer it." Honey jumped up and grabbed her shirt.

—

Judith hadn't thought the whole thing out. She hadn't planned for that third party. It's one thing to make a scene with your own husband, in the privacy of your home, where one doesn't have to worry about protocol and bad manners. But to be greeted by a puzzled young woman, a child really, and one who clearly was in an advanced stage of undress; that was truly daunting. What was the appropriate response? How did one express oneself correctly and with dignity yet still get the message across?

The girl stood in the doorway, frozen in panic and fear. Judith could see August fumbling with his pants over by the sofa. She could also see her vase there on the table.

"Excuse me," Judith said. "I'm Mrs. August Wentworth. Is my husband here, by any chance?"

The girl looked over her shoulder towards August, as if he could save her from this moment.

"I'm coming, Judith." August walked to the door.

"My vase," Judith said.

The girl had backed into the room and was hovering over by

the TV. August walked over to the table and picked up the vase.

"Leave the flowers," Judith said. She didn't want those things in her house. Lilies were ruined forever.

August carefully lifted the flowers out of the vase and handed them to the girl then carried the vase to the door.

"Do you have a key?" Judith said.

August reached into his pocket, pulled out a single key and handed it to her.

"Not to me, you fool," Judith said.

August turned and offered the key to the girl. She walked over and took it out of his hands.

"Young lady," Judith said. "You will never see my husband again." She pulled August out the front door, closed it, then led him forcefully down the stairs, away from the apartment building.

22

It's Time to Give Honey Her Break!

*J*ack was feeling good. He was well rested and completely over the flu. Time to make a move. Now or never. He'd been driving around for a while, looking for a parking spot. It was impossible in this neighborhood. Then Jack saw an elderly man climb into a shiny black Bentley and start the engine. Excellent, right in front of Honey's building, the stars were definitely in alignment today. The old guy went back and forth a few times trying unsuccessfully to maneuver his big boat of a car. There was plenty of room but depth perception and agility must diminish with age, poor guy. Jack considered getting out and helping the old fellow but he finally got the nose of the car pointed in the right direction and drove away. Jack didn't know how much one those Bentleys cost but he figured he could probably live comfortably for a good five years off the price tag. He quickly pulled his truck into position and parked.

The knock on the door was shy, tentative. Did Gus somehow sneak back? Doubtful. Gus hadn't been exaggerating; Judith

Wentworth was the scariest woman Honey had ever seen. That look. That voice. There was no doubt in Honey's mind that Judith could erase her very existence in the mere blink of a well made-up eye. She was not going to let that husband of hers out of her sight.

Honey had just finished cutting the top off a half-gallon carton of milk to make a vase for the flowers. They looked stupid but she didn't want to throw them away. The flowers were pretty and maybe the last nice thing she would have for a long, long time. She had no money and the job at the diner was not enough to pay the bills. Gus had been her only hope. The knock came again, this time more insistent. Honey put the flowers on the table and went to answer the door.

⸻

Jack tucked his faded work shirt into his jeans. He ran his fingers through his hair to make it stand up all wild the way Honey used to like it. He couldn't let himself think about how it would be when she opened the door. He wouldn't even allow himself a plan. He'd knocked and now, if she was home, he'd take whatever she wanted to give him.

⸻

Honey opened the door. He stood there, exactly as she'd been picturing him for all these years. His tanned face was harder, leaner than before but somehow more handsome. And those eyes, could they be any bluer? He smiled but Honey couldn't move. Was this real? Was Jack Belmont really standing in front of her or was she just making it up? Honey had seen a show on the TV where victims of trauma sometime hallucinate alternative realities in order to escape their current situation. Had Judith Wentworth thrown Honey into a waking dream starring Jack Belmont?

"Honey?"

He spoke. Honey couldn't remember from the show if the hallucinations could actually talk.

"It's me, Jack."

He wasn't saying anything too complicated, surely her wounded brain could come up with a basic greeting. There was only one solution here. She had to touch him. She had to find out if Jack Belmont was real. Honey reached towards him. She fully expected her hand to pass right on through this beautiful mirage of a man but it was stopped by his iron-hard stomach. She looked in his eyes and he smiled again. She brought her other hand to his chest, feeling his warmth through his shirt, the tightness of his muscle, then she wrapped her arms around him as he pulled her close and bent to kiss her. It was like the first time, all over again.

"I'm sorry, Honey." Jack kissed her neck then pulled back slightly and looked into her eyes. He reached up and tucked a stray hair behind her ear. "I fucked up."

23

Judith and August— A New Beginning

*J*udith drove home with both hands on the wheel. She was careful to observe the speed limit: 25 mph residential, 30 once she got to the commercial area. As she drove she realized that while she lived in a huge metropolitan city, it might as well have been a small town because she rarely ventured outside of her insulated community. Really, there wasn't any reason to leave the neighborhood. Everything she needed, all the necessities and luxuries, was within a five-mile radius. These different areas, the less fortunate environs, seemed foreign to her and may as well have been in another state all together. Santa Monica, Culver City, Mar Vista, Beverlywood, they had absolutely nothing to do with Judith's day-to-day existence and made her feel somewhat ill at ease. But she relaxed as she finally pulled onto Sunset, the street that would deliver her home.

August was back there in traffic somewhere. She hadn't bothered to wait for him. She needed this time to figure out exactly how she was feeling, what she wanted to do. That scene had been a terrible ordeal. Dreadful. Absolutely humiliating, something from which a weaker person might never recover. But Judith was nothing if not strong, very few things in life that Judith Wentworth couldn't handle. Still, there was no denying that this was one of those pivotal moments.

———

Exhausted. That's how August felt when he finally got his car out of the tight parking spot in front of Honey's apartment and headed towards home. He wanted to curl up in a ball and sleep. There would be hell to pay with Judith, she would probably punish him for years. He would like to sleep through that. He was tired, tired of trying to prove he was a man, tired of worrying about his ability in the bedroom, tired of sneaking around. He just wanted to go home and crawl into his bed.

———

Judith pulled her car into the garage and turned off the engine. She had to decide, right now, what it was she wanted. Of course August would have to pay for this ridiculous escapade but the question was, how much? She could throw him out. When he pulled into the garage, she could order him upstairs to his room and tell him he had exactly thirty minutes to pack his bags. She could call the locksmith and have the house re-keyed, change the code on the alarm. Yes, with very little effort she could banish her husband and start a life free of August Wentworth and his shameful behaviors. Is that what Judith wanted? To go through with some sort of nasty divorce? It would be in the papers, of course, all that money, the Wentworth name. It would be the number one topic of conversation at all the dinner parties across this city for years to come. August and Judith Wentworth, divorcing after forty-five years of marriage. August and his serial infidelities. Poor Judith. She would have to give up her membership at the club. It would simply be too awkward for them both to belong, socialize at the same place. The Lloyds had attempted that and poor Lillian was humiliated when Bernard started dating Elise Stone. No, Judith would have to leave the country club forever. And what about their friends? Who would side with whom? Judith knew the answer, everyone would side with August. He was the source of all this wealth, the power. When in doubt, people always went with the money. That would leave Judith volunteering at various charitable organizations around the city with all the other divorced women in Los Angeles. She had no illusions, women her age didn't find love again. Even with money, there were just too many sweet young things waiting to swoop down on men like her husband. Did Judith really want to walk this earth alone for the rest of her days? No, that was definitely not the life that Judith Wentworth had signed on for.

—

"You're not to do that, ever again."

"No."

"Ever."

"I swear."

"And you'll stop drinking."

"If that's what you want."

"We'll get Dr. Stern to help. Or Dr. Thompson. They've got pills for it, I think."

"All right."

"Did you put the vase back?"

"Right where I got it."

"Is it still wet?"

"Don't think so."

"Because if it is, I'll have a lot of trouble getting those water marks off later."

"Do you want me to go check?"

"Yes."

"I'll be right back."

"Use a clean dish towel."

"Will do."

"And bring me some mint tea."

"Mint tea. Anything else?"

"Chocolate. There's some in the pantry. Bring the whole box."

———

August went down to the kitchen. He didn't know where the dishtowels were kept but just as he was about to press the bell to summons one of the maids, Rosa, came running from the laundry room.

"You need a dish towel, Mr. Wentworth?" Rosa quickly opened a drawer and handed him a freshly ironed towel.

"Thank you," August said. He was puzzled but didn't have the energy to ask how she'd known.

"Should I make some tea?" Rosa was already filling the kettle with water.

"Yes, tea." August said.

August went into the butler's pantry and got the vase down. He polished it over and over, rubbing hard, trying to release that genie that would grant him peace. When he was sure there were absolutely no marks or even finger prints on the glass, he replaced it on the shelf and returned to the kitchen. Rosa had a tray prepared with tea and a box of chocolates which August carried upstairs to his wife.

24

The Itsy Bitsy Spider is a Brown Recluse

Angela was crouched in the bushes outside of Conrad's house. It was a dark cold night and she'd been waiting over an hour. She hadn't planned to be here but somehow couldn't stay away. How would Conrad respond to her note? Would he fly into a rage, break things? Would he pace the floor, pulling his hair out? She'd never seen him lose control. She wanted a glimpse of who he really was, one true moment. She wanted to see him shatter, grind his teeth and howl at the moon.

Conrad's flight landed at 8:30 Thursday evening. It had been his intention to go straight home from the airport, get a good night's rest after the long, taxing trip. But then blond-haired, big titted Tiffany Dushay bent over his seat and offered him a cocktail, served him dinner and finally sat next to him during the movie. She told him her interminable life story but gave him a good look at her tight long legs by letting her skirt ride up. Conrad changed his plans. She was young, maybe twenty-five and very beautiful in that cheap flight attendant way. An ambitious little digger looking to lay a claim but sexy as hell. Now they were in the back of the limo headed to his house and as Conrad leaned in to kiss her, he found that he was not feeling the least bit tired.

"I've never done anything like this before," Tiffany whispered.

"I know." Conrad unbuttoned her flight attendant blouse and extracted a surprisingly pink nipple from her cheap, black lace bra. "Me neither." He licked his fingers and twisted the nipple back and forth. She ran her hand over his crotch, then moaned when she found his rock hard erection. She went for his belt buckle with a healthy enthusiasm but he stopped her. They would be home in another couple of minutes.

The car pulled up in front of the house and they got out. Conrad told the driver to take the car around to the side and wait. This was not going to be a long evening; he had an early breakfast meeting tomorrow, plus he didn't like women to spend the night, especially on a first date. He opened the front door for Tiffany and punched in the code for the alarm. She made noises about how beautiful his house was, tiresome babble, so he kissed her to shut her up. They stood there in front of the huge plate-glass window, pressing their bodies together. She had a very firm ass and Conrad gave it a good hard slap just to see how she'd respond. She appeared to like it because she stuck her tongue deep into his mouth then went to work on that belt buckle. Conrad hit her again and she moaned. Excellent. She unzipped his pants then sank to her knees. Conrad smiled. If this little girl wanted to skip the prelims and blow him right here in the entry hall, fine with him. He could take care of this and get that good night sleep after all.

❧

Angela hadn't expected him to show up with a girl. That was a real fly in the ointment, certainly a distraction. Angela crept a little closer to the big window. She watched as the girl unzipped Conrad's pants and knelt in front of him. He was staring out the window, exactly in her direction, but Angela knew he couldn't see her there in the dark. What was that look on his face, certainly not joy. He looked tired, maybe even bored? Angela smiled. He'd never been bored with her. The girl got to work and Conrad ran his fingers through her long blond hair then grabbed two big handfuls and worked her head back and forth on him. That's what he always did with Angela, weird watching their private routine acted out with a stranger.

⚊

I should have brought my jacket, not the leather Versace, the Ralph Lauren with the fur lining, cuffs and hood. And gloves. It's freezing out here. But how was I supposed to know that Miss Angela Simms is a full-blown night stalker? Look at her over there crouched in the bushes watching my big brother get a very uninspired blow job from that little stewardess. I should open a school. I'm a very gifted teacher, you know. THE NORMAN WENTWORTH CENTER FOR THE STUDY OF ORAL SEX? *We guarantee to turn you ladies into expert fellators in two weeks or your money back.* What do you think? Heterosexual women would flock to me from around the country and heterosexual men would deem me a hero. I'm sure August would bankroll it. Go global, make millions.

Oh, shhhh. Angela's making a move. She's creeping forward, commando style, through the hydrangeas. Trying to get a better look? I wonder if this is part of their routine, "Showtime" in the entry hall. I doubt it. I don't think there is an Angela/Conrad routine any more.

Well, would you look at that? Conrad just shot jism all over that nice girl's face and hair. Damn that didn't take long, couldn't have been more than three or four minutes. Maybe my brother isn't quite the player I thought he was. They have medication for the premature ejaculation problem. I'll bring it to his attention at the next family dinner.

⚊

Conrad watched as the stewardess made a big show of enjoying the fact that he'd come all over her face. She wiped her cheek then sucked her fingers. Yummy.

"There's a bathroom right through there." Conrad pointed down the hallway. "Go clean yourself up."

The stewardess look confused, a little hurt, but recovered quickly. She stood and Conrad saw that she had a nasty run in her panty hose. "Be right back," she said and walked down the hall, working that sexy ass, but Conrad wasn't interested anymore. She'd served her purpose and he was ready for her to go now. Wouldn't it be nice if you could just press a button and make them disappear?

The stewardess came out of the bathroom all fresh and ready for round two. "Do you think I could maybe have a drink or something," she said.

Conrad shook his head apologetically. "Not really in the cards tonight." He put his arm around her shoulders and gently herded her towards the door. "I've got an early meeting and I'm exhausted from the flight. You must be too." He got to the door and opened it.

"Wait." The stewardess seemed to be having trouble deciding between pain and rage. "What do you mean?"

Conrad took her arm and with just the slightest amount of pressure, pulled her down the front steps. "You're great," he said. "Beautiful. And I'm looking forward to getting to know you. Really, I am. Just not tonight."

"So I'm like, dismissed?" The girl pulled her arm away from Conrad and stood her ground at the bottom of the steps. Conrad whistled for the car and the driver pulled up front.

"Just tell Randy where you want to go." Conrad opened the car door. "He'll drop you anywhere."

"You can't..." The stewardess didn't want to be loaded into the car so Conrad gave her a little push as he forced her body inside.

"I'll call you tomorrow," he said and closed the door.

The stewardess opened the door and said, "You don't have my number, asshole."

"Give it to Randy," Conrad said. "Talk to you soon." He gave a little wave of his hand then slammed the door. The car took off before she could argue.

—

Wow, that was cold, huh? Even for Conrad. Can you believe he and I share a genetic history? He didn't even kiss her goodbye. You want to always end on a high note, leave the door open for the future, just in case. It's just good strategy. I would teach that at my school and the world will be a much nicer place if people would heed my lesson.

Look, he's reset the alarm and is heading upstairs. Surely we can go home now. I mean, what can Angela possibly be hoping to see once he goes to bed? He's turning off all the lights, for God's sake. Perhaps I'll reveal myself once she gets back to her car. We could go for a nice coffee at the House of Pies or something. I will be her shoulder to cry on, offer up invaluable advice. She needs me.

—

Angela didn't intend to go inside. That was crazy; she could get herself shot. But when Conrad shut down all the lights and she lost access to him, she found she couldn't tear herself away. She just had to see what he would do when he found that note. She had to be a part of it.

—

It was obvious to Conrad that someone had been there. The books that obscured the video library were sitting on the table and he could see that several tapes were missing. He rushed into the bathroom to check the safe but it seemed to be untouched. The .44 Magnum was still in the drawer next to the basin. He grabbed it. Whoever the fuck had been here was going to pay. He returned to the bedroom and that's when he saw the panties and the note there on his pillow.

—

I'm telling you, this girl is insane but very impressive. Sneaking up the steps and opening the front door? I am positive Conrad didn't give her that key. Now she's disarming the alarm. A regular James Bond. And the good news is that it looks like she's left the door ajar. So, what am I going to do? Well, I'm not going to sit out here in the freezing cold when the show's clearly happening inside. Besides, she's probably going to need backup when that lunatic brother of mine realizes Fort Knox has been invaded. Norman Wentworth to the rescue.

———

Angela crept up the stairs. She was slightly disappointed not to hear Conrad ranting and raving. He could at least throw a vase. But it was quiet. She knew he was in his bedroom because of the light. Had he found the note? Of course he had, it was right there on his pillow. What was he going to do? What was she going to do? Angela had no idea. She reached the top of the stairs and crept down the hallway towards his room.

———

Conrad set the gun on the bedside table and put the books back in their place. There was a part of his brain that was able to appreciate Angela's plan, a tiny piece of him even admired her stupid courage. This was insane. Did she really think she could black-mail him? What, threaten to go public with the tapes unless he marry her or pay her off? How about he just *knock her off* instead and they could call it even?

He sat on the bed and took off his shoes. What the fuck did he care if she went public with those tapes? There wasn't much on them: straightforward sex, a little gentle torture. Those twins were young but good luck finding them. They were probably working some labor camp in Cambodia by now. He pulled his shirt off and threw it on the floor. Did Angela really want her naked ass shown all over town lapping it up with her girlfriend Alison (maybe she did)? But whatever, that wouldn't hurt him. He'd performed well in that little movie, if memory served.

Conrad stood and took off his pants. He thought he should

probably shower, wash the spit off his cock, but he was tired. The shower could wait until tomorrow. The only real problem was Rusty Goldman's daughter. A big can of worms, that one. Very bad judgment on his part to film her, even worse to show it. What had he been thinking?

He went to brush his teeth. Sweet little Bethany Goldman. She liked sex as much as any full grown woman he'd ever met. In fact, a case could be made that she'd instigated the whole thing, calling him at the office all the time, showing up at his house. He'd practically had to fight her off and a man can only be strong for so long. It had been going on for a couple of years. Just last week she'd called to say she finally got her braces off and asked to come over, even offered to bring one of her girlfriends. No, this was not good. He had to get that tape back. Conrad splashed some water on his face and dried himself. He looked tired. He was tired. He switched off the light in the bathroom. He could deal with this tomorrow.

———

Angela brushed the dirt from her knees and did her best to smooth her hair. She wasn't nervous. She should be. This was very dangerous. Crazy. Conrad had a very bad temper. But Angela felt calm or maybe she was just numb. Where should she be? Standing in the middle of the room? Hiding in the closet? Seated in the chair by the fireplace? Lying on the bed? And should she be smiling? Angry? Sexy? (No, that little stewardess *ho* had eliminated the sexy option for this evening plus she wasn't really dressed for it.)

———

Conrad wasn't surprised to see Angela standing there in his bedroom. Nothing this bitch did surprised him. It was too bad he was naked, too bad the gun was over on the table, because he did feel just a tad vulnerable.

It's the *Animal Kingdom* starring the hyena and the lamb only lamby-girl is a hybrid-freak with viper teeth and a rattly tail. If she spits in his eyes, he'll go blind—toxic venom like the world's never seen. Conrad has no idea what he's dealing with. They're standing on opposite sides of the room, staring each other down. Any minute, I expect to hear hisses and growls. Conrad is naked. Just as I always suspected, he's not nearly as well endowed as I am. His flaccid penis is so sad, don't you think? Small and pathetic. When you see him here, like this, you realize he's really not much of a man. Kind of makes you feel sorry for him, doesn't it? I mean, you wouldn't exactly hold him up as an example of fitness, vigor and health. Even for his age he's very soft through the mid section and a little droopy in the rear. I will never let myself go like that. I promise you. Never! I'd rather die.

We're going on a good minute and a half, are they ever going to speak? Each of them is calculating the odds. My money's on Angela. I'm standing here, tucked behind the door, and I've got a perfect view of the entire room. Look, you can tell Conrad wants to cover his feeble manhood but he's fighting the urge, probably thinks it'll make him look weak. Are those goose bumps? I think our girl is actually making him nervous. Here we go, Angela's making a move. She's pouncing like the fierce lioness that she is. Oh God. Oh no.

Angela grabbed the .44 Magnum. It was very heavy and so she held it in both hands as she aimed it at Conrad. There wasn't really a "gun plan," she'd never fired one in her life, but when she spotted it her survival instinct dictated that she keep it away from Conrad.

"Put the fucking gun down Angela." Conrad took a tentative step in her direction. This crazy bitch could be dangerous. Fear made him suddenly cold and he could feel his balls pull up into his body. He had to get control. "Drop it, NOW."

—

It made Angela mad that Conrad thought he could tell her what to do. How dare he? She got to call the shots now; she earned it. And so she swung the gun over towards the doorway and pulled the trigger. The gun kicked back at her and blast was much louder than anticipated. Her ears rang. "Back off, motherfucker," she yelled, exactly like a Brooklyn cop, then she re-aimed and pulled the trigger again. The television exploded in a million pieces. "I will blow your head off," she said. "Don't make me."

—

Norman wet himself. The first bullet exploded into the door just inches above his head and his bladder released. His pants were drenched but it could have been much worse. His bowels held tight and somewhere, deep in the back of his mind, he congratulated himself for having such good control. He crouched down. Fight or flight? Fight or flight? He huddled with his eye glued to the crack in the door, paralyzed.

—

Conrad just stood there, looking at the hole in the wall where his TV had been. Little twat. She broke into his house, stole his stuff and now she had blown up his plasma television, which had cost a fortune. Conrad clenched his fists, all fear evaporated into rage. He looked at the skinny bitch. She was mean, capable of a lot of nasty things, no doubt. But she didn't have the balls to shoot him. No way.

—

Angela did not have time to think. Conrad was flying through the air in her direction, hate spilling out all over the room. She saw that he would kill her if she let him, so she aimed the gun right at his head and pulled the trigger just before he got his hands around her neck. What surprised her, what really seemed strange, was that his head did actually seem to blow off. Not that it was completely gone, part of the left side was intact, the cheek and ear, but enough of it exploded that you could make a case that his body was in fact headless. What a mess. Angela herself was covered in blood and little chunks of meat and bone. Who would clean up something like this up?

———

Norman could have stopped this. He could have said something, prevented Angela from entering the house, yelled out a warning to let Conrad know what was going on. He could have done almost ANYTHING and his brother would be alive. But no. He had sat there, hiding behind the door, watching. He enjoyed drama, had hoped something bad would happen. Norman fed on other people's problems. Norman the voyeur. Man on the sidelines. Mr. Vicarious Thrill. Perv. It was the story of his entire life and this is what it led to.

He watched as Angela attempted to wipe the blood and gristle from her tangled hair. Medusa. How could he have ever sympathized with this woman? Norman wanted to kill her now. The monster that took his brother and for what? He wanted to stand up and grab her and slit her throat, watch her die on the floor right next to Conrad. He wanted to make her pay. But as she wiped the gun clean of her fingerprints and grabbed the note and panties sitting there on the bed, Norman found he couldn't move. She scanned the room for evidence and Norman sat very still. He was having trouble breathing. She grabbed her purse. Tears welled in his eyes. Why couldn't he just stop her? Say something. She walked out of the bedroom but Norman didn't move. The fucking bitch. He sat there, huddled behind the door and didn't make a sound as she ran down the stairs and escaped.

25

911

"Mom."

"How dare you, Norman. It's eleven o'clock at night. What are you thinking of, calling so late?"

"Mommy?"

"Oh. Oh no. Dear God, no. You've been arrested again, haven't you? August wake up. Norman's in jail."

"No. Mom. Mommy. I'm not in jail. I'm . . . I . . . I need . . ."

"You're drunk. You have no right to awaken me in the middle of the night . . ."

"NO. It's. . . . You need . . ."

"On drugs then. You know how I feel about drugs. August, take this phone. I can't deal with your drug addict son."

"Norman, what's wrong?"

"Dad. She shot him and his head is in a million little pieces like Humpty Dumpty only with blood and brains and little bits of scalp with hairs. She ran out and I can't make my legs work so I'm still behind the door where I was hiding. I should have stopped it."

"Who was shot?"

"I couldn't stop her. Or maybe I could have, but she's gone."

"Stop babbling and explain yourself."

"Angela Simms. She killed Conrad and now she's gone. And Conrad can't fix it like he always does 'cause he's dead so I think you're going to have to come over here and fix it yourself 'cause I seem to be broken."

26

Aftermath

The fire was burning in the living room although Judith didn't remember asking anyone to light it. It was three o'clock in the morning. There were sandwiches laid out on the table, tuna and egg with the crusts removed, and coffee. Was Rosa responsible? Judith didn't know. What did it matter? August was lying on the couch with his hand over his eyes. Surely he couldn't be sleeping although it certainly did look like sleep. Becky was balled up in a chair sobbing while Paul patted her on the back and whispered reassurance. The sound was annoying and Judith would have preferred it if they had stayed home. She just wanted quiet. There was nothing to be done here and Judith didn't particularly feel like taking care of anyone else. At what point do adult children stop being the parent's obligation? Must one care for one's offspring until the day that one dies? What a tremendously depressing thought. Conrad had been the only one of her children who had fully matured. The ideal son. Considerate, loving, kind. HE took care of HER. Now she was left with a bunch of needy, dependent people. There was no justice in this world, a world in which Conrad Wentworth would be taken and Norman Wentworth left behind. Yes, it was a terrible thing to think. But it was true!

Judith did not shed a tear. There was no room for weakness. She had gone with August over to Conrad's house and met the police. The paramedics had Norman out front on a stretcher by the time they arrived and the house was a crime scene, no one allowed inside. The body, Conrad's body had been taken away. Where did it go? Judith couldn't remember what the man said.

Norman was a blubbering mess. He'd wet himself and seemed incapable of completing a sentence. Judith had ridden in the ambulance with him to the hospital. She knew she should have offered him some sort of comfort, held his hand, smoothed his forehead, but somehow she couldn't. They'd ridden in silence, Norman dozing from the sedative. August signed the commitment papers. Judith couldn't think about what came next.

27

Breaking News

—

$\mathcal{T}$*he Beverly Hills Bugle*
—Breaking News—
Thursday, March 14
Beverly Hills, California

Crime of Passion Leads to Life of Vice:

PROMINENT ATTORNEY BRUTALLY SLAIN IN BEVERLY HILLS MANSE: Evidence at the Scene Points to Victim Conrad Wentworth's Possible Sex Crimes

By: Jamie Thompson

The body of prominent Los Angeles attorney Conrad Wentworth was discovered Tuesday night in his home in Beverly Hills. Sources within the Beverly Hills Police Department confirm that he had been shot once in the face at point blank range.

Police were summoned to the scene at 10:45 pm Tuesday by a frantic 911 call from the victim's younger brother, Norman Wentworth, who was apparently a witness to the crime. The body of Conrad Wentworth was dis-covered in the master bedroom of his luxurious Beverly Hills mansion. Police do not consider the younger Mr. Wentworth a suspect at this time.

Norman Wentworth reportedly claimed his brother was shot at approximately 10:00 p.m. Tuesday night after an altercation with a jeal-ous ex-girlfriend. An APB for an Angela Simms was put out by the BHPD at 11:00 p.m. but the suspect remains at large.

Police department sources will neither confirm nor deny the appar-ent discovery of a large collection of bondage sex paraphernalia and ille-gal drugs found at the scene as well as an extensive personal video collec-tion that links the victim to sex crimes involving minors. A full investi-gation is underway.

Steven Monclair, an attorney for the Wentworth family, said that they had no comment except to deny any wrongdoing on the part of the victim.

Conrad Wentworth is the son of August and Judith Wentworth and the grandson of prominent Southern California real estate developer Edward Wentworth. He is survived by his parents, and his siblings Norman Wentworth and Rebecca Wentworth-Jones, his niece Monica Wentworth-Jones and nephew Joseph Wentworth-Jones. Mr. Wentworth was never married and has no children.

The Wentworth family is responsible for developing Eastwood, the town of Many Oaks, and a large section of the Seminal Valley. They are considered one of the foremost philanthropic families in this city.

28

Lay it to Rest

$\mathcal{B}$ecky didn't want to wear black to her brother's funeral. Navy, gray, those were appropriate colors, weren't they? And what was wrong with yellow, exactly? Or pink? Purple and orange? She sat on the floor in her closet looking up at all the choices. Becky had a lot of dresses.

"Sweetheart," Paul said. "What are you doing on the floor?"

"Black is ugly," Becky said. "Never gonna wear black again. Get rid of all these dresses." She pointed up at the left side of the rack. "See Paul?" She turned her head and looked up at her husband. "Black, black, BLACK. Trash."

Paul tried to pick her up by the armpits. Becky went limp. She didn't want to stand. She was happy right where she sat, in her cozy closet. Becky tipped over and spilled out of his arms onto the floor then curled into a ball.

"Becky," Paul said. "We have to leave for your parents' soon." He got down on his knees and tried to prod her into a sitting position. "The funeral. You've got to get up."

"Kinda like spaghetti, huh?" Becky said.

"What?"

"Me." Becky giggled but she did not sit up. "Slippery spaghetti."

"How many pills did you take, sweetheart?"

"I have no idea what you're talking about." Becky giggled again. She was feeling so relaxed and just a tad bit sleepy. This would be a perfect place for a little nap. A naplet. Nappy pie. Night-night, pajama face. Shhhhh Mommy's sleeping.

Paul walked into the bathroom and opened the medicine cabinet. There were a couple of prescriptions on the shelf, mostly stuff for his postnasal drip. One bottle of sleeping pills for Becky, practically empty. Paul grabbed the sleeping pills and emptied them into the toilet then began his search in earnest. She'd been doing so well. He thought her drug problems were behind them. But now, faced with a real problem she slipped right back into her old ways. What kind of model was she to the kids? It made him mad. Enough was enough. He checked under the sink but found only towels. He checked in the drawers. Where would Becky hide her drugs? Paul spun around and went back to the toilet. Of course. The Tampax box. Paul had always been somewhat squeamish about the woman's monthly cycle, even the thought of blood made him vaguely nauseous, and so feminine hygiene products were something that he made a point to steer clear of. But now he opened the box and there they were: Zanax, Valium, Adavant, Clonipin. Four different doctors, one of them Dr. Rosenblatt. He emptied all the bottles into the toilet and flushed. This was the end. If she had to check into one of those centers, so be it. He would not allow his wife to continue down this path.

Paul switched on the espresso machine in the kitchen and ground the beans. He didn't really believe that caffeine was going to sober her up, but what other choices were there? They had to be at the parents' house in an hour.

Paul carried the espresso back into Becky's closet. She was still curled into a ball on the floor, sleeping. He looked at her. There was a wet spot on her arm where she had drooled.

"Becky," he said. "Wake up." He kneeled, careful not to spill the coffee, and gently shook her shoulder. "Sweetheart, I've brought you an espresso."

Becky jerked up like some witchy-possessed jack-in-the-box and swatted the cup out of Paul's hand. "I don't want any fucking coffee, pighead."

Paul snapped. There was a ringing in his ears and a strange, but not unpleasant, metallic taste in his mouth. He drew his hand back and slapped his wife across the face. It wasn't full force, he could have hit her harder, but it was enough that she fell back, stunned. Paul's hand tingled from the impact.

"Get up," he said.

Becky just lay there looking at him. Paul expected her to fight back, he was ready for her omnipresent rage, her screaming and yelling, perhaps a physical assault. Bring it on. But Becky did not seem the least bit angry. She laid there, on the floor, hand to her cheek, and stared at Paul with, what? Astonishment?

"I said, get up." Paul turned and selected a dress, black Jil Saunders, sleeveless with a belt. It was one of Paul's favorites and perfect for the occasion. "You'll wear this and you will behave yourself."

Becky stood. She accepted the dress. "Okay."

"You will take a shower. Cold shower." Paul took her arm and led her into the bathroom. "You will pull your hair into a neat ponytail, there's not time for you to style it."

Becky nodded as Paul turned on the water. He added a little hot. He wasn't a cruel man. Then he took off his clothes and pulled off Becky's bathrobe.

"You will be respectful to everyone." Paul guided Becky into the barely warm shower. "No more scenes. Understand?"

Becky nodded. She dutifully stood under the spray and allowed him to wash her back and shoulders. He forced her to stand under that chilly spray for a good three minutes then turned off the water and helped her out.

"It's hard on everyone, Becky." Paul patted her dry with a big fluffy white towel. "Not just you."

"Okay." Becky stood still, waiting for her husband to continue.

"You will behave yourself." Paul handed her the black dress. "We're doing things my way from here on out."

29

Dearly Beloved

*J*udith didn't know how to handle the Goldman family. One couldn't exactly write a note of condolence lamenting the fact that one's son had taken terrible advantage of their teenaged daughter. She was sorry, desperately sorry, the whole thing made her sick, but did the family really want to hear from her? Luckily Judith had never met the Goldmans, even though the father was a partner at Conrad's firm, and so maybe she didn't have to address the issue at all.

It was hard to reconcile the boy she had raised with the man she read about in the papers. When Judith closed her eyes she still saw Conrad as a beautiful adolescent running up the beach with his surfboard, smiling and waving. He'd been such a good boy, hadn't he? Such a loving son. She couldn't think of him that way now. She couldn't think of Conrad at all or she wouldn't survive this. She had to block him out completely. One day she'd deal with this. One day when she was stronger.

Judith received endless calls of sympathy from friends. They all started out saying how sorry they were for the terrible loss and then wheeled around to the scandal. Everyone wanted to hear what Judith had to say. What was there to say? The terrible details of Conrad's very sick personal life were in every paper on both coasts. She could tell her friends that the man they described was not the son she knew. She could imply that the press had exaggerated. But the Goldman girl had come forward and admitted everything to the court-ordered psychologist. August made arrangements to pay for her long-term therapy. Judith couldn't exactly deny that these things had happened. There had been no exaggeration. Conrad Wentworth, her son, had been a monster.

In some ways the scandal was a help. It didn't allow Judith to feel. It acted as a barrier between herself and the pain. Conrad was gone and the rest of the family was left behind to deal with his mess. It was Judith who would have to somehow restore dignity to the Wentworth name. How she was going to accomplish this was anyone's guess. It would take time, but that was the job she had to focus on now. Maybe someday in the far off future, when the world had moved on and forgotten, maybe then she would have time for her grief. For now she had to finish getting dressed.

August sat on the bed in his under shorts and socks. He knew he had to get dressed, knew that the family would arrive any minute, but he couldn't seem to get himself to stand up and walk to his closet. What suit was he supposed to wear to his eldest son's funeral? What shoes? Those decisions seemed far too difficult, decisions that he shouldn't have to make in this lifetime, and so August sat there. Waiting.

Judith walked in and looked at him. She came and sat next to him on the bed, took his hand in hers and squeezed. Then she leaned over and hugged him. He took her in his arms and held her. Maybe they could just stay there, sitting on the bed, holding each other. Maybe that's all they had to do. Just sit together and rock, back and forth.

Judith kissed his cheek then stood and left the room. He felt a chill, missed the heat from her body. She returned a minute later with his suit, shirt and shoes. He stood and she helped him get dressed.

———

Paul led his family through the front door and into the living room. Judith was still upstairs getting ready, August was sitting on the couch drinking a glass of soda water with lime. He smiled at Paul but didn't stand, nor did he speak. Paul got his family situated, Becky next to her father on the couch, Joey and Monica on the matching chairs. Becky had sobered up a lot. She seemed in control and was even attempting to comfort her father so Paul excused himself to use the restroom. He made a quick detour to the butler's pantry where he replaced the missing silver tongs with the rest of the tea service. Finally. It was such a relief to get rid of those things. He'd felt like he'd been holding his breath for weeks. No more secrets, ever again. If Judith asked, Paul was prepared to tell her exactly what had happened. They would deal with it as a family.

———

Joey watched his dad come back into the living room. It was cool. He didn't have any use for those stupid tongs anyway. It had been almost two weeks since Joey had taken anything, not that he didn't want to sometimes, but the stealing really upset his father. His dad smiled at him and he smiled back.

———

Judith walked through the butler's pantry on the way to the living room. She stopped. The tongs. The tongs were on the tray next to the sugar bowl. Someone had returned the tongs. Someone had stolen her tongs and now, for whatever reason, that same person, or perhaps a different person, had decided to return them to her. Someone in this house. Someone in her inner circle. All this time they'd kept her tongs and now they'd decided to return them. Judith's mind started to wander over the list of possible suspects but she stopped herself. The hell with it. What did it matter now?

Judith grabbed the tongs and wrapped them in a dishtowel. She opened the bottom cupboard and stuffed them way in the back corner where no one would find them. She would deal with the tongs another day. Or maybe she wouldn't.

———

Norman was quite comfortable in his hospital bed. He liked the crispness of the sheets, even though they were a cotton blend, and the fact that they would change the bedding anytime you wanted. He liked the simplicity of the room: the TV, the rolling nightstand, the blue plastic pitcher of ice water and matching cup. He felt safe here. He liked his psychiatrist too. Dr. Stuben had a very gentle voice and soft hands. She touched him on the arm or hugged him when he cried. He felt safe with her and so when she'd asked him if he was ready to go home, ready to attend his brother's memorial service, Norman had feigned a relapse. He didn't want to leave this place, ever.

There was a drawing pad and some colored pencils on the table. The staff had been encouraging Norman to draw, whatever came to mind. He'd been working on a series of caterpillars, inching along on thin delicate branches. They were nice drawings, he could see that, and he'd given a couple away to the nurses who cared for him. The drawing soothed him. He picked up his pad and pencils. Today was his brother's funeral. Today Norman was going to put the caterpillar into a cocoon.

———

Grandma announced it was time to go. Monica watched her grandpa stand up from the couch. Her mother held his arm as he navigated around the coffee table and headed for the door. He'd never seemed old before but today he was ancient, so frail. All of them were fragile, like they might break at any moment. Judith walked out the front door, followed by Paul and Joey. Monica stepped up and took her grandpa's other hand. Together, Monica and her mother led him out to the waiting limo.

30

Epilogue

The Section at the End of the Book
That Serves as a Conclusion to What has Happened.

Angela Simms was taken into custody just outside of Battle Mountain, Nevada for the murder of Conrad Wentworth. She had changed her name to Mary Wells, dyed her hair black and was wearing fake reading glasses and a prosthetic nose but that didn't stop the good citizens of B.M. from recognizing her and collecting the million dollar prize money that was offered after she was featured on the hit TV show, *Find that Felon*. She put up quite a fight and the deputies had to shock her with the taser gun in order to secure her in cuffs and leg shackles. It seems that Angela was much stronger than they anticipated and in fact inflicted several painful bites on the forearm and left shoulder of the commanding officer, one of which bled and required medical attention. They took her down to the station, booked her and threw her into a holding cell with a couple of tough prostitutes from Lovelock, NV, where she spent a torturous night that culminated in a tragic miscarriage which necessitated a lengthy hospital stay before she could be transferred back to Los Angeles in order to stand trial. Angela was convicted of first-degree murder and sentenced to a life behind bars. She is now trying to settle in at Chowchilla

Women's Facility where she is being encouraged to explore her lesbian tendencies.

The Happy Helpers Preschool was leveled and is now the site of a full service day spa. Most of the parents relocated their children to the nearby Circle of Learning Preschool but not all of the families could be accommodated and that caused a tremendous amount of stress for those who were left out. The Blossom Center for Early Growth took up most of the slack but the rejection that those families felt caused a lot of damage and some of those kids will never be the same.

The Belmonts jumped into Jack's truck and headed out of Los Angeles. Their plan was to drive until they found a spot that all three agreed upon, somewhere beautiful with fresh air and open space. In the course of their journey, Jack and Honey were officially married in a little church near Big Sur. Kimmy was the flower girl. They eventually settled in an area of Ukiah, off Highway One, on a street called Happy Lane. Jack was able to buy a nice little house, with the money he'd inherited from his mother, in an area that had an outstanding school system. Kimmy really blossomed with the attention of her daddy and excelled in all areas of learning. She's now reading at a fourth-grade level even though she's still in preschool and she has tremendous ability as a musician, specializing in both the tuba and the violin. Jack and Honey renewed their incredibly fulfilling sex life and enjoy each other at least twice a day; in fact Honey is now pregnant with their second child, a boy, due in July.

Rosa the housekeeper bought a lottery ticket at the Shop 'n Go market on Fairfax and won the second largest jackpot in the history of California. After sorting out some legal troubles, she returned to Guatemala where she purchased a big house in an upscale part of the city and has enrolled all her children in private school. She hired a housekeeper and a cook but treats them with nothing but respect and they adore her. She's found a new man, Antonio, who treats her like a queen and they plan to marry in July.

Maggie Halliburton, the widow of August Wentworth's best friend David Halliburton, published her first novel at the age of 66. She'd been writing for years but never told a soul, other than David, and it was only after his death that she felt ready to let her work be shown. The book was snatched up by Overlook Press, after a fierce bidding war, and is a runaway bestseller. It deals with the themes of love, family and loss. Maggie spends most of her time doing book tours and talking to large audiences about her inspiration and work process. A major studio has bought the movie rights and Johnny Depp is set to play the lead.

Dr. Rosenblatt has taken a leave from his practice. He was forced to sell his house in order to pay off the divorce and is living on a rented sailboat in Marina del Rey. He is currently working on a series of relaxation audiotapes that utilize guided imagery and song and hopes to begin marketing them in July.

The loss of Conrad was a tremendous blow to all of the Wentworths and the resulting grief is a burden under which they all will struggle for years to come. However, life goes on:

Judith and August left the day after the funeral for a three-month grand tour of Europe. Judith used the missing tongs as an excuse to scour the best antique shops on the continent. They found an exquisite tea set that was far superior to the original.

August stopped drinking except when Judith felt like a glass of wine, then he joined her. During the trip he discovered that chocolate acted as an aphrodisiac on his wife and so he spent his free time in search of the world's finest truffles. Judith gained a little weight and it had a surprisingly positive effect on her face. She looked five years younger with the added ten pounds, plus she found herself in an amorous mood most of the time. Sex became a pleasant activity for Judith and August and, for the first time in their lives, they actually enjoyed each other's company.

Paul and Becky also discovered a very rewarding sex life. It turned out that Becky responded quite favorably to bondage and light discipline. She particularly liked to be "hog-tied" and spanked with a ping-pong paddle. And, surprisingly, Paul found that he was quite good at dominating his wife. He took up racket ball, an aggressive sport at which he excels, while Becky enjoys the soothing aspects of Tai Chi. Becky weaned herself off prescription drugs by taking constant shots of wheat grass juice and flaxseed oil. She has never felt better in her life.

Shortly after the funeral, Monica turned her sights towards college. She's hoping for a small liberal arts school on the East Coast. Her first choice is Vassar with Wellesley a close second. Joey overcame his need to steal through the support of his father and joined the chess club at school. He has really come out of his shell and is one of the better players. There's talk of nominating him for team captain in the fall.

Norman finally received the psychological counseling he so desperately needed. In the course of his therapy, he took up painting and has proved to be a remarkable talent. No one knows it yet, but he will go on to become a world famous artist who will go down in history as one of the great painters of all time. His work will hang in museums around the globe. You will find him in all the art books; your grandchildren will study his work.

Also by Katie Arnoldi

Chemical Pink
978-1-59020-083-4

"A dazzling first novel—entirely original, dizzyingly controlled, all ice-cool momentum on the surface and all shock below."　　　　　—JOAN DIDION

"A modern gothic comedy of obsession."　　　　　　　　　—*Vanity Fair*

"One of the most unusual pieces of fiction I've ever seen. I read it non-stop in 4 1/2 hours; couldn't put it down. Comic and horrifying, sadistic and hilarious, tragic and funny all at the same time. . . I never read anything quite like this. It's as if the Marquis de Sade got loose again with his funny bone banging at our front door."　　　　　　　　　—LIZ SMITH, syndicated column

"It is difficult these days to shock and beguile with a kind of aggressive innocence, but Miss Arnoldi has in this book. It is disturbingly funny and utterly unflinching."　　　　　　　　　—SUSANNA MOORE, author of *In the Cut*

 The Overlook Press New York www.overlookpress.com